Of Shame and Joy

LAWRENCE BLOCK
writing as Sheldon Lord

OF SHAME AND JOY

LAWRENCE BLOCK writing as SHELDON LORD

Copyright © 1960 Lawrence Block

All Rights Reserved.

Cover and Interior Design by QA Productions

A LAWRENCE BLOCK PRODUCTION

CLASSIC EROTICA

21 Gay Street
Candy
Gigolo Johnny Wells
April North
Carla
A Strange Kind of Love
Campus Tramp
Community of Women
Born to be Bad
College for Sinners
Of Shame and Joy
A Woman Must Love
The Adulterers
The Twisted Ones
High School Sex Club
I Sell Love
69 Barrow Street
Four Lives at the Crossroads
Circle of Sinners
A Girl Called Honey
Sin Hellcat
So Willing

THE SICK ROSE

O Rose thou art sick.
The invisible worm,
That flies in the night
In the howling storm:

Has found out thy bed
Of crimson joy:
And his dark secret love
Does thy life destroy.

—William Blake
Songs of Experience

CLASSIC EROTICA #11

OF SHAME AND JOY

Lawrence Block

CHAPTER 1

The beach was empty. The sun was hot on the water and hotter on the white sand that stretched wide and pure and shining in the sunlight. The tide was ebbing, receding slowly but steadily to reveal shells and starfish and still more sand.

It was a perfect day for the beach and the beach was the perfect sort of place for that sort of day. Hot, hot enough to vaporize lead, but not sticky or muggy. A dry heat, a baking heat, with not a cloud in the sky and a slight and gentle breeze that kept the air fresh and sweet smelling.

It was such a perfect day for the beach, as a matter of fact, that it seemed strange that the beach was as empty as it was. But this particular beach was fairly well removed from the mainstream of life, a good half-hour's drive from Provincetown. While beaches closer to the town were crowded, and while beaches farther up the cape were dotted with people, this one beach at this one time was completely empty.

Until the girl came.

The girl came by herself. She drove up in a year-old Ford convertible, a pale green car with whitewall tires. She left the car in a parking lot that had been empty before she arrived and made her way down to the water with a huge yellow beach towel in one hand and a bathing cap in the other. Halfway to the water she changed her mind suddenly and sprinted back to the car, leaving the cap on the front seat. She ran back to the water once more, spreading the towel out on the sand near the water's edge and racing full-speed into the surf.

The water was cold at first, freezing cold, and it sent shivers racing over her flesh. When she was in water halfway up her thighs she stood for a moment with her arms crossed over her breasts and each hand gripping a shoulder, trembling a little with the cold. Then she steeled herself and ducked beneath the water.

At first it was a tremendous shock. Then, after she began swimming around with a lazy breaststroke, the edge of the cold was dulled and she was able to enjoy the physical pleasure of being in water on a hot day. She swam out a ways, her arms moving effortlessly in the rhythm of the breaststroke, her legs working in an automatic frog kick. She loved swimming, loved the taste of the salty ocean water when she caught an accidental mouthful, loved the feel of the water below her and the hot sun blazing down on her.

When she was out far over her head she rolled over onto her back and floated. At first the sun hurt her eyes through her eyelids but after a while she stopped noticing it and let herself relax completely.

She floated for ten or fifteen minutes. Then she rolled over again and began swimming, this time in a fast and furious overhand crawl. She swam back to shore much more speedily than she had swum out, but again her movements were perfect and easy and her body knifed through the water with a minimum of effort.

On shore again she pressed the water from her long ash-blonde hair, wondering for a moment if it might not have been a good idea to wear the bathing cap after all. She decided that it didn't much matter any more, that whether the milk was spilled or not there was no sense crying over it.

For a long moment she stood motionless in the sun. The wet black bathing suit was sleek against her body and her skin was golden from previous exposures to the sunlight. She was a tall girl with the sort of figure all tall girls ought to have and so few do— long and willowy, with full hips and fuller breasts that pushed persistently at the top of the swimsuit and threatened to leap out into the sunlight at any minute. Her legs were perfect in the way that only a tall girl's legs can be perfect.

She was a lot of woman. A lot of beautiful woman.

With the breeze playing with the wet ash-blonde hair, with the sun shining on her and the wet swimsuit looking as though it had been painted on, with nothing around for miles but white sand and blue water, she was almost too beautiful to be real.

After a moment or so she sat down on the towel, then stretched out full length on her back. The sun felt good, so good, and she wanted to let it bake all the wretchedness and pain out of her body. She lay very still for a moment; then she sat up suddenly and looked around.

There was nothing to see.

She hesitated for several minutes. She wanted to peel the wet suit from her body and let the sun hit all of her, toast her whole body a pleasant shade of brown. But suppose someone should come and see her there, all naked and unprotected and exposed? Was it worth the risk? The beach wasn't private even if it was deserted, it wasn't her own private beach where she could do whatever she pleased. For that matter, there was probably even a law against nude sunbathing. Suppose someone should come as she had come while she was sleeping nude in the sun?

Well, so what if they did? She laughed bitterly, thinking that anybody who hadn't seen her nude already deserved the chance. If some son of a bitch came to spy on her he could stare at her until his eyes fell out and it wouldn't bother her, not really.

Why, it wasn't as though she was a sweet little virgin who had never been touched by a man.

It wasn't like that at all.

She drew herself to her feet, reaching awkwardly behind her back to undo the suit. The movement drew her breasts tighter against the front of the swimsuit and made her all the more anxious to get it off. The hook-and-eye attachment was a minor headache, the zipper was a major one, but after a few more seconds the suit was off and lying limp in one corner of the towel, while she was stark naked and lying just as limp in the center of the towel.

Golden flesh on a yellow towel on a white beach under a white-hot sun.

The area covered by the swimsuit was lighter in hue than the rest of her. During the winter she took occasional sun-lamp treatments, but her breasts and belly were still less tanned than the rest of her skin. She worried for a moment or two that the hot sun might burn her breasts, and the thought of the skin peeling from her breasts alternately sickened and amused her. The breasts themselves didn't appear at all wary of the sun. They stood firm and proud and large and conical, thrusting pink nipples to the sun like rosy offerings to an angry god.

Her eyes were closed, her body completely relaxed. The

physical exhaustion of the swim before made it easy for her to lie limp and motionless; the heat of the sun on her nakedness made relaxation very pleasant. For a moment or two thoughts filled her mind, some of them not particularly pleasant. But it's hard to think unpleasant thoughts on a beach with the sun warming you, and it wasn't long before her mind was as empty as a mind could be and her head swimming lazily in a sea of warm perfume.

She slept.

The Mayflower cast anchor in Provincetown Harbor on November 20, 1620. There is a marker at the west end of Commercial Street, one of the two streets which run the length of the town, which marks the first landing place of the Pilgrims. Before them one Bartholomew Gosnold landed near Provincetown in 1602 and named the whole cape, calling it Cape Cod because he had seen a whole store of codfish. Before him there were Norsemen, before them the Indians.

For years Provincetown was a whaling center next only to New Bedford and Nantucket. Now the whaling ships are long gone, but the principal industries otherwise remain what they were since the seventeenth century—the catching, curing, packing and selling of cod and mackerel. At Provincetown men still go down to the sea in ships and come home smelling, like Mister Snow, of fish.

There is, however, one important addition to the list of local industries.

It is the tourist trade.

The population of Provincetown varies between around 5000

and over ten thousand, depending upon when you count noses. In the summer, when the sun is always hot and the beaches always white and the dunes invariably beautiful, tourists from all over the country, chiefly Boston and New York, flock to the Cape Cod beaches. Some of them stop at Hyannis, the commercial center of the cape, a dull and uninteresting sort of a town. Others go to Falmouth or Buzzards Bay or any one of a number of towns. A good many wind up in Provincetown.

They find places to live, accommodations ranging from one-room ramshackle hovels in the woods to multi-room suites in fairly expensive hotels, from trailer parks to cottages to rooms with private families. They include ad men and insurance sales-men and steelworkers and college students and honeymooners and divorce-celebrators, with a heavy proportion of artists and writers and a much heavier proportion of would-be artists and would-be writers. They come alone or in pairs or in crowds, and they stay for a weekend or a week or a month or a season.

They swim in the sea or the bay. They soak up sun on the beaches. They take pictures of the dunes and watch plays at the Provincetown Playhouse and drink from Pilgrim Spring and watch the sunset at Race Point. They talk to the Town Crier, and around 35,000 of them take his picture every year. They watch artists paint pictures and listen to folksingers sing folk-songs. They devour thousands of clam rolls, spoon thousands of bowls of clam chowder down their throats, rub thousands of bottles and jars and tubes of various and useless suntan lotions into their skins, and otherwise enjoy themselves. The ones who come in couples make love with renewed vigor in the warm, dry, refreshing climate; the ones who come alone have little difficulty in finding bed partners of the opposite sex, or of their own sex, depending upon their particular inclinations in that area.

They have a good time, evidently. There are more of them every year.

Greg Tyler was a tourist. When he wasn't occupied with the business of being a tourist he was a businessman on a small scale. He had a sporting goods store in Worcester, a natural occupation for a man who had played football and baseball and basketball in college and who didn't have the stuff to make it as a professional in any of the three sports.

He stood well over six feet tall, with broad sloping shoulders and sandy hair cropped close to his skull in a boyish crewcut that preserved the college boy look of him. He was ordinarily quite light in complexion, but constant exposure to the sun had turned his body a deep nut-brown. His eyes were blue, a very clear blue, and his firm chin looked as though it had been chiseled from granite.

He was unmarried and he liked it that way. The sporting goods store brought him in enough money to live very comfortably single and not comfortably at all if he had to support a wife as well as himself. He lived alone in a bachelor apartment near the store and worked more or less when he wanted to. When the fish were biting he would close the store and load tackle in the trunk of his battered Plymouth. When he spent a night in glorious dissipation he didn't have to feel guilty if he elected to stay in bed until afternoon. And, when the full force of July heat hit Worcester and covered it like a smelly blanket, the Plymouth could take him to Cape Cod and the store could go to the devil for the time being while he found himself some sun and sand and sea and solitude.

Which was why he happened to be at Cape Cod.

Which was why he happened to be at Provincetown.

Which was why he happened to be at a beach that afternoon.

And which was why he happened to be staring with frank admiration at the naked, sleeping form of Sheila Paine.

Perhaps she heard his breathing subconsciously. That may have been why she was aware of his eyes on her body without opening her own eyes. It was very strange: one moment she was sound asleep; the next moment she was still motionless but completely awake and completely aware of his presence. At first she was afraid. Then she was embarrassed. Then, finally, she was curious to see just who it was who was staring at her body.

She opened her eyes.

She saw him before he saw that her eyes were open. His eyes at the time were dividing their attention between her breasts and her thighs, and he didn't have much time for the rest of her. He was standing just a foot or two away from her and she took her time looking him over, taking in the hard muscles in his arms and legs and shoulders, the unutterably frank blue eyes, the barrel of a chest set on top of the narrow waist. While she was automatically angry at him for staring at her, her pulse involuntarily quickened at the sight of him above her, looking so virile and handsome and so obviously approving of what he saw.

She said: "38-25-37."

He actually jumped.

"What—"

"My measurements," she said thinly, still lying inert with only her lips moving as she spoke. "You seemed curious, so I thought you might like to make note of the statistics. You can jot it down in your diary and mull it over on cold nights when you don't have anything better to do."

He took an involuntary step backwards, trying to divert his eyes from her body but having a tough time of it. His mouth opened and he started to say something but no words came from his lips.

"Stop gaping," she said. "You might have the decency to turn and look at the water or something."

He turned and looked at the water.

"That's better."

"I'm . . . I'm sorry," he stammered. "I just came down here for a swim and you were here."

"Yes," she said. "I was. I still am, for that matter. So are you."

"I—"

"I'm not blaming you," she continued. "It was my fault. This is a public beach and if I had the nerve to take my suit off I deserved to get looked at, or seen, anyway. But I don't think it was particularly nice of you to go on staring at me like that."

She was beginning to enjoy his embarrassment. It was hard to tell under all that tan, but it seemed to her that he was getting red in the face.

"I'm sorry," he said.

"Sorry?" She raised one eyebrow neatly, but the gesture was hidden from him because he was still contemplating the water quite intently.

"I couldn't help it," he said thickly.

"Sure."

"I mean—"

"You mean that you never saw a woman quite like me before—is that it?"

"I—"

"I hope that's not it. That's such a tiresome line, and I should hope you'd be able to come up with a better line than that one."

The red, or what seemed to be red, spread to his neck.

"Look," he said, "I'll get out of here, okay? I'm sorry I had to stare at you like an idiot, but I'll go now."

He turned and began walking off, and her eyes were glued to his broad back as he walked. She wanted to close her eyes tight but her eyes stayed the way they were. She wanted to relax again, but every muscle in her body was firm and tense and rigid and she knew that she couldn't relax, couldn't possibly relax, not until something was done that she didn't really want to be done at all.

Damn it, she thought. Damn it to hell.

You promised, she told herself. You promised up and down that there wouldn't be any more men and it never did a damned bit of good. There was a man, and he looked at you, and the next minute you were ready to spread yourself and welcome him like a long-lost brother.

Damn it, anyway.

"Wait a minute," she called.

He stopped in his tracks.

"Come back here."

He turned around and walked toward her, careful to keep his head turned and his eyes gazing down at the sand by his side.

"Look at me."

"What the—"

"Look at me," she repeated.

He looked at her. At first he tried to confine his gaze to her face, but what he saw in her eyes made him travel the length of her perfect body with his eyes, paying careful attention to every feature of her.

It was an optical rape. The way he was looking at her sent familiar sensations coursing through her body. There was the gentle but insistent tingling in her arms and legs, the almost pleasant lightness in her head, the pounding of her heart and the spreading, searing warmth in her groin.

Damn you, she thought. Damn you to hell.

"Do you like what you see?"

"Yes," he said. "I like what I see."

His voice was husky.

"If you like it so much, why don't you do something about it? You shouldn't just stand there doing nothing."

"What do you mean?"

"Don't you know?"

He didn't answer.

"Do something," she said. "Damn it, don't just stand there like a dummy."

"Here?"

She was beginning to find it difficult to breathe and even more difficult to lie still. Her hips were itching to start moving, grinding against him. Her mouth wanted his mouth against it. Her whole body was aching for him.

"Of course here."

"But—"

"But what?"

"Somebody might come."

"Somebody already did. You."

"But—"

"If anybody else shows up," she said positively, "he'll just have to wait his goddamned turn."

He got his suit off, his fingers trembling. He stepped out of the red swimming trunks and left them in the sand.

He joined her on the towel.

The second his hand touched her bare shoulder her arms were around him, gripping him, pressing him tight against her and holding him close. She burned a kiss against his lips and pried his mouth open with her hot red tongue, not afraid of being the aggressor but only interested in him, in the closeness of him, the nearness of him, the musky man-smell of him and the strength of him. She wanted him, wanted him hungrily and desperately, and nothing was going to stop her from having him.

She could feel the hairs on his chest as her breasts pressed against them. His arms were like a vise around her back, a vise that grew tighter the more she probed his mouth with her demanding tongue. Then the vise loosened and one hand began stroking the smooth skin that was as smooth as a newborn baby's, cupping her and touching her and driving her into a frenzy.

His teeth found her lower lip. He bit her, gently at first and harder the second time.

His breath was hot on her face, his heart was beating as fast as her own was, and she could see beads of sweat on his forehead and upper lip.

Then his mouth covered hers and she couldn't see anything at all.

The sun burned like an inferno in the cloudless blue of the sky. The nubby towel was damp with her sweat as their bodies writhed together upon it. The world stood off to one side, silent except for the steady and persistent lapping of the waves against the beach.

And, finally, it was over.

She held him for a long time. Then her arms fell to her sides and he slipped away from her. They remained silent for a long time, unable to say anything.

Finally he said that his name was Greg Tyler, and she replied that her name was Sheila Paine.

That seemed to be the end of that.

After awhile they dressed. They sat around some more, talking a little from time to time and staring at the sea the rest of the time. They went for a swim and she was pleased to discover that he swam as well as she did. They swam far out in the ocean, floated for awhile, and returned to shore.

She did not reach orgasm when they made love.

Sheila Paine had never reached orgasm in her life.

Chapter 2

The Purple Oyster was located at the corner of Bradford Street and Standish Street. It was a small café, just a hole in the wall really, with the Bizarre Gift Shop to the right and Dos Manos Fried Clams to the left, a cozy cubbyhole with small round marble-topped tables and wire-backed cane bottom chairs.

Harvey Chase, the slim dark young man who owned and operated the Purple Oyster, sat in the rear behind the small counter and waited for business. It was late afternoon, beach time and perfect beach weather, and at that hour on that sort of day the Purple Oyster was generally closed while Harvey was lying on a beach in the sun. But this particular day he hadn't felt like sun or sea, and as a result the Purple Oyster was still open.

Unfortunately, few of the regulars realized that the café was open and fewer still seemed to care. At one table a boy named Morton Hume was talking earnestly to a girl named Dolores Metakowski. At another table an old regular with a white beard sat by himself, his nose buried in a slim volume of imagist poetry and his lips moving as he mouthed the words silently to himself. His first name was Peter, and if he had a last name no one in Provincetown seemed to know what it was.

There was only one other customer in the Purple Oyster. She, like Peter, was seated alone. She was not reading, however. She sat by herself, her eyes centered upon the surface of the white marble table top between her small white hands. She didn't move, didn't raise her eyes, and you had to look closely to see that she was breathing. A glass of iced cider rested on the table top at her elbow but she did not so much as touch it, and the ice cubes melted into the cider in the electric heat of the afternoon.

The girl was very attractive. Her hair was jet black with a bluish cast to it and so vivid that the coloring seemed as though it must be artificial; it was real enough, however. Her eyes were large and brown and their lashes were long and graceful. Small but perfectly formed breasts pressed against the front of a plain white blouse that was almost severe in its simplicity. Her Bermuda shorts were a plaid with red and green predominating, and they revealed pretty knees and excellent legs. On her small feet she wore white tennis shoes with no socks.

The girl was small, small and dainty, with every feature in perfect proportion to the rest of her. If she had stood up, she would have stood just a hair over five feet in height; seated, her diminutiveness was not quite so apparent.

For a long time she made no movement whatsoever. Then her face contorted into a frown and she glared at the spot on the table top. Her brow was knit with concentration and the muscles and tendons in her forearms went taut. Then, after a moment or two, her pretty face relaxed into a slight smile and the corners of her mouth turned up slightly.

The girl wrapped the fingers of her right hand around the glass of cider and lifted it to her lips. Her fingernails were unpainted and her lips unlipsticked. She sipped the cold cider, taking a sip that was small in keeping with her own size. The she put the glass down once again on the marble table and stared at the same spot between her two hands.

The girl's name was Madelaine Carr.

Bruce Ryerson was, all things considered, a rather medium person in appearance. About five-nine in stockinged feet, with a face that was handsome but featureless, an attractive face that was actually quite uninteresting because it looked as though it had been stamped from a mold. It looked like the face in the men's shirts advertisements, an ordinary face, a standard face. Perhaps if he had borrowed the eye-patch from the shirt ads he would have looked more distinctive. As a matter of fact he had considered affecting an eye-patch at one time, but he gave it up in short order.

Bruce Ryerson was a native of Provincetown. He lived there twelve months of the year, working five days a week as a clerk in the town's one book shop. It was an easy job, with next to nothing to do in the off-season and little enough to do when the tourists were out in full force. Tourists bought books, true, but tourists only bought so many books and did so mainly on rainy days. The book shop showed a nice profit, but there were never tourists breaking down the doors in order to buy out the shop, and Bruce Ryerson had what was generally known as a soft touch.

What made the touch a good bit softer was the fact that the Maple Hill Book Shop was owned by one Samuel Ryerson, who happened to be Bruce's father. This made things infinitely simpler. If Bruce wanted to take time off, all he had to do was tell his father that he was taking time off. It was as easy as that.

Bruce liked Provincetown. In the winter it was something of a drag from time to time, but even in the winter there were women around, women who were often willing enough to be put to the use which Bruce wanted to put them to.

And in the summer Provincetown was a satyr's paradise. While Bruce wasn't quite a satyr he was quite definitely an operator, and a good-looking woman tossing her hips against his was his idea of heaven.

This afternoon he was not working. It was too damned hot to work, he had decided, and he had informed his father of the fact. His father agreed with him completely, so completely that he not only gave Bruce the afternoon off but closed the shop himself and went home to relax with a pitcher full of dry martinis.

Which was why Bruce happened to be walking downtown on Bradford Street.

He had a glass of grape drink at the Havadrink Stand on the corner of Bradford and Arch. He gobbled a clam roll at Dos Manos Fried Clams.

He almost walked right on by the Purple Oyster.

Something made him turn his head. He glanced through the small window for just a second; then he stopped dead in his tracks.

He saw Madelaine Carr.

He liked what he saw.

She was, he decided, quite lovely. She was also quite alone, and quite obviously not waiting for anybody in particular. Since he felt it was almost sinful for a pretty thing like her to be sitting alone in a pleasure town like Provincetown, he thought it might be a decent thing to join her.

He stood outside on the sidewalk, snapping his fingers noise-lessly and getting his approach straight in his mind. If he was go-ing to make a pass at the girl he wanted to do it just right, and he sure as hell didn't feel like muffing it. It had been three days since he had made love to any woman at all and almost a year since he had made love to one anywhere nearly as attractive as Madelaine Carr.

Finally he had the bit straight in his mind. The door to the Purple Oyster was wide open and he walked through it, walking directly to Madelaine's table, his legs moving in a firm and con-fident stride. There was one other chair at her table and he sat down in it directly across from her. She looked up, startled, and he gave her a huge smile and settled one hand on the marble table top an inch or so from hers. His smile widened as he saw the look of shock and surprise in her large eyes.

His approach was, to say the least, unusual.

"I'm sorry I'm so late," he said. "I hope you haven't been wait-ing too long."

She just stared at him.

"I got tied up," he said. "I would have been here earlier but we ran into a snag at the shop."

Her eyes narrowed. "I'm afraid you have made something of a mistake," she told him, her words carefully spaced and flawlessly enunciated, her voice soft and smooth as mellow cornsilk.

"A mistake?" His eyes sparkled.

"I don't know you," she said, "and you don't know me. If some-one was waiting for you here, I'm afraid they have left. At any rate, I'm quite obviously not the person you're looking for."

He was unperturbed. "I'm Bruce Ryerson," he said, irrelevantly.

"Is that supposed to mean something? I'm afraid I don't know anybody named Bruce Ryerson."

"You do now."

For a moment she regarded him strangely. Then her eyes flared.

"You're not only a clod," she said, "but you are also a relatively unimaginative clod with an inordinate amount of unadulterated nerve. I have nothing to say to you and you quite obviously have nothing to say to me. Now that you have introduced yourself I'd consider it a personal favor if you'd leave me and find some other individual to annoy."

"Whew! I just wanted to say hello—"

"You've said it," she snapped. "Now go away."

"What's the matter?   Somebody spike your Red Heart?"

"Your conversation," she said coldly, "is as amusing as your personality is stimulating, and I'm afraid I must report that I find you totally uninteresting in both respects."

"I don't get you."

"Precisely."

He was shaken up and annoyed. While he had had passes tossed back in his face often enough—you always did if you tried often enough—he had never gotten a response quite like this one. The smile still on his face and the sparkle still present in his eyes, he took her small hand in his and looked into her eyes with what he imagined was a soulful expression.

She drew her hand away as if he had leprosy and glared hard at him.

"What I really wanted to say," he began, ignoring the look in her eyes, "is that there's this party tonight over at the Hookery and I'd like you to—"

"Mister Ryerson."

Her voice stopped him cold.

"Mister Ryerson " she said again, "I seem to have failed to make my point. If you don't get up from that chair this instant and leave me alone I am going to kick you square in the crotch."

She watched him until he was out of the door and on his way down Bradford Street. Then she relaxed visibly and went limp. She put her elbows on the table and rested her face in her hands, half wanting to cry but unable to do even that.

God, she told herself, you're a wreck. For God's sake get a grip on yourself.

With an effort she raised her head and took another sip of the cider. All the ice had melted by this time and the cider was a lukewarm mess with a sickly sweet smell to it. She put it down, swallowing the little she had sipped and making a face as it trickled down her throat.

The nerve of that clod, she thought. A person couldn't even sit by herself without one of the local yokels trying to get her into a bed. Wasn't it obvious that she wasn't interested? What did she have to do—wear a "hands off" sign or something?

Maybe that would be the answer—a sign. No more headaches like Bruce Ryerson, not if she had a sign on her back. The sign would make everything perfectly clear, even to a moron like the one she had just disposed of, that the lady was simply not in the mood.

What would the sign say?

That was easy to figure. That was relatively simple, if you just gave the matter the least bit of concentrated thought and attention. Without much difficulty you could sum up everything in one word.

One word would do it.

Just one word, one simple, short, easy word. With that word on her back all the Bruce Ryersons in the world would step aside to give her a wide berth. Nobody would bother her any more, not when she was wearing her sign like an armadillo wearing a coat of armor.

One word.

A nice word, really. A soft and pleasant word, a word she hated once but a word that she now was rather fond of.

One word.

Lesbian.

She stood up, pushing herself away from the table. She walked easily to the counter in the back of the Purple Oyster and paid Harvey Chase thirty-five cents for the glass of iced cider, then turned and left the Purple Oyster and walked out onto the street.

The sun was still hot, the sidewalks still relatively empty of people. She walked quickly, the mental sign riding easily on her small back, proceeding up Bradford Street to Daggett Lane. Mrs. Hadrian's Rooms for Rent was located at 41 Daggett Lane between Bradford and Commercial, a massive white frame house in traditional New England architecture. Madelaine opened the screen door, said hello to no one in particular, and climbed the slightly winding staircase to the second floor.

Her room was small but pleasant, with a keenly polished hardwood floor and well-made unpainted furniture. The bed was solid and the mattress hard the way she liked it. She undressed rapidly and hung her clothing over the back of a chair. Then she flung the one window wide open, enjoying the cool tangy ocean breeze on her bare skin.

She stretched out on the bed, still a little furious with Bruce Ryerson, still a little angry at herself for her own vulnerability. The mattress was firm beneath her, the pillow soft and fluffy under her little head.

She slept.

And remembered . . .

She was born in Boston, the only child of Nathan and Anne Carr. Like the song, her father was rich and her mother was good-looking. Her father bought and sold real estate, buying it for a good deal less than he sold it, and the three of them lived in a massive stone house in one of the better sections of Boston.

In keeping with the Carr money and the Carr social position, Madelaine was sent to a private high school in southern New Hampshire as soon as she had graduated from grammar school. That might have been the greatest mistake—there were times when she thought she might have been "normal" if she had gone instead to a public high school in Boston. Other times she was certain that her lesbianism would have asserted itself in any case.

But the private school made things that much easier. It was a school for girls only, girls like Madelaine, girls with money and good family backgrounds.

Girls like Lita Barnstable.

Lita, with dark red hair the color of polished chestnuts. Lita, with bulging breasts and muscular thighs.

Lita, who was the first.

When Madelaine was a freshman Lita was a sophomore, and already Lita had been initiated to the shadowy pleasures of lesbian love. Madelaine, on the other hand, had about as firm an understanding of sex in any form as she had of differential and integral calculus. She knew what the books told you—that men and women married and copulated and created children. She knew that there was supposed to be something pleasurable about the process but she didn't see how it could be enjoyable in the least. The thought of a man doing *that* to her was somehow disgusting and sickening.

She got to know Lita slightly that first year. Lita would talk to her in the hallway, sit next to her in the lunch room. Lita's eyes frequently examined her body with a frankness and intensity and admiration that should have been unmistakable, but which Madelaine never understood at the time.

"Maddy," her roommate told her once, "I think you ought to stay away from that Lita Barnstable."

"Why?" Madelaine wanted to know.

"I've heard that . . . well, that she's different."

But the hint was lost on Madelaine Carr. *Different* meant many things, but to her it didn't even suggest what her roommate was attempting to convey.

It was during her second year and Lita's third year that the two girls became genuinely close. For one thing, it was easier for a sophomore and a junior to be good friends than for a freshman and a sophomore. With the added year the difference in age became less significant. For another thing, Lita's lover had graduated in June of the previous year. The older girl was restless, hungry, yearning for love.

And Madelaine was young—and ready for love.

They danced together at a school dance—that was the first remotely physical contact between the two. The private school was fairly well isolated and boys could only be imported on special occasions, so girls dancing with girls was an accepted part of the program. Madelaine had danced with a good many girls, but dancing with Lita was a good deal different. She could feel how tight Lita was holding her, and every once in a while Lita would pull her in close and their breasts would touch, Lita's large breasts pressing urgently into Madelaine's small breasts, Lita's thighs taut and rigid against the younger girl's.

She was very confused for several days afterwards. She was quite mixed up—for the first time in her life her body and mind had been stirred by sexual desires and she was too young and immature to recognize those desires for what they were. She was vaguely ashamed without being sure what it was that she was ashamed of, vaguely worried without knowing what was frightening her.

Two days later Lita kissed her.

It happened in Lita's room, with Lita's roommate out for dinner and Lita's door tightly shut. They were sitting together on Lita's bed, and Lita felt the hunger building up within her until she couldn't resist it any longer.

She stopped trying.

She took Madelaine's chin between the thumb and forefinger

of her right hand and brought Madelaine's mouth to her own. Madelaine felt a pair of lips pressing against her own lips, soft, seeking lips. Then Lita's arms were around her back, holding her in close so that their breasts were pressed tight together.

Lita's lips forced her own lips apart and she was suddenly tasting the almost overpowering sweetness of Lita's mouth. Lita's tongue invaded her mouth and slipped past her parted teeth and lit little fires wherever it touched.

She was breathing hard now, intoxicated by the passion of brand-new feelings, brand-new sensations. Lita kept kissing her, kissing her mouth and her eyes and her cheeks and her forehead and the tip of her nose, and Madelaine's head began to swim.

It was Lita who ended the kiss. She broke away and drew back sharply, her eyes worried and her lips parted.

"God," she said. "Oh my God!"

Madelaine didn't say anything. She didn't know what she was supposed to say.

"Maddy—honey, do you have the slightest idea what's going on here?"

Madelaine shook her head. Lita said *God* again and jumped to her feet. She found a book at the back of the bookshelf over her desk and handed it to Madelaine.

The book was *We Walk Alone* by Ann Aldrich.

"Read this," Lita ordered, her voice tense and throaty. "Go away from me now and read this from cover to cover, and don't see me until you've finished it. Then, if you want, come to me."

Madelaine read the book that night. She read it in bed under the covers with a flashlight, read it all the way through at one sitting, and after she had finished she hid the book away in her desk drawer.

She couldn't sleep.

She knew, knew with an awful certainty, what she was and who she was. Now her feelings for Lita were easily intelligible, easily understandable, obvious and elementary.

She went to Lita the next night.

Lita undressed her. There was a chair propped under the door knob to make it impossible for anyone to enter the room and the window shade was pulled all the way down. Lita undressed herself after she had stripped the clothes from Madelaine's firm young body, and then the two girls lay down together on Lita's bed.

They kissed and they touched and they cried. They made love, and it was the first time, and it was perfect, absolutely perfect, and Madelaine's whole body sang with the special joy of a woman in love with a woman.

The following year they roomed together. Then Lita graduated and went to college halfway across the country and Madelaine thought she would die.

But she didn't die.

Instead she found somebody else.

There were more, many more. There were two more girls at the private school and many more girls at Colby Junior College where she went after she graduated. Then she was expelled from Colby when her attachment to another girl was discovered. Her parents were informed and once again she thought she would die.

And once again she didn't die.

Her parents were sick and disgusted with her. But she was still their daughter and they were willing to support her on the condition that they didn't have to see her and be reminded of their shame. Boston was a huge city, and it was possible for Madelaine to have a fine apartment of her own and all the lovers she wanted without ever running into Nathan or Anne Carr or any of their friends or relatives.

And there were more girls. She didn't work; she didn't go to school. Now she was twenty-four years old, spending her first summer at Provincetown.

And she needed a woman so badly that her groin ached with the need for love.

CHAPTER 3

Sheila Paine drove the pale green Ford convertible into town on Highway 6. Then Highway 6 conveniently turned into Commercial Street. She followed Commercial as far as Howland and turned right, driving past Bradford and into comparative wilderness.

She parked the car in a segment of wilderness that was cleared to form a sort of a parking lot and climbed out of the car, locking it behind her. Theoretically it wasn't necessary to lock anything in Provincetown—a car or a house or a chastity belt was supposed to be safe without protection of lock-and-key or Pinkerton men or the Secret Service. But Sheila Paine didn't believe in trusting anybody unless it was absolutely necessary. She never left her car door open unless she happened to be in the car. She never left her small cottage without locking the door behind her, and never went to sleep in the cottage without sliding the bolt into place.

Since she didn't feel that a chastity belt was particularly essential in her case, she didn't have one to lock.

With a deep breath of woodsy air in her lungs she began walking toward her cottage. The Buchanan Shanties were all set a good ways away from civilization and it was a healthy hike from car to cottage. She stumbled her way to the cottage over a path which seemed to have remained untouched since the Battle of Hastings, either because of Buchanan's desire to retain the rustic pleasure of the area or because of Buchanan's reluctance to spend a cent on improvement.

After she had unlocked the door of the little two-room shack and stepped inside she was almost able to relax. She sat down in one of the rustic wooden chairs, thinking that *rustic* seemed to be a synonym for *decaying* in the Buchanan thesaurus, and surveyed the cottage through a pair of tired blue eyes.

The cottage, she decided sadly, had been badly misrepresented by Mr. Buchanan's neat little folder that winged its way to her shortly after she requested travel information from the Province-town Chamber of Commerce. Not that there were any downright lies in the folder—it was just that Mr. Buchanan had a knack for describing something and making it sound a good deal better on a printed page than it actually was.

Spacious living-room. If you could live in very little space, the living room was spacious. *Frontier-style kitchen.* Well, that was honest enough. All the grubby little hole needed was can-dle-molds and a foot-warmer and you'd swear you were back in colonial days.

Colonial-style furniture. Now there Buchanan had under-stated his case. The *style* was not necessary. The furniture in her cottage was quite obviously genuine colonial furniture, stuff the Pilgrim Fathers were careful to leave behind when they left Prov-incetown for the comparative shelter of Plymouth. Why, they just didn't make beds that sagged like hers did, not any more. And they hadn't been able to make chairs quite so uncomfortable as the one she was sitting in since Jefferson bought Louisiana.

Oh, the hell with it. There was no point in knocking the cottage—for one thing, she was glad to get back to it this time. For another, she had to put up with it for the remainder of the season and it made sense to make the best of it.

For a third, it was taking her mind off what she was supposed to be doing. She was supposed to be mad at herself, and how could she scold herself properly if she took out all her aggressions on poor old Mr. Buchanan?

The chair was too uncomfortable to think straight in and she transferred herself to the sagging bed, lying squarely in the middle of it so she would sag evenly. She kicked off her shoes, stared for a moment or two at the unpainted wooden ceiling with the rafters showing, and then began to swear softly at herself.

"Damn you," she whispered fiercely. "Damn you for being such a sex-hungry little bitch."

Well, she told herself in reply, could she help it if such a good-looking hunk of man had to appear while she was taking a private sun bath?

Yes, she answered back. He was ready to leave. You didn't have to call him back.

Oh, everything was going wrong. The whole point of the Provincetown vacation had been to get away from men for a change, to give herself a chance to change a little. There was something radically wrong with her, and men like Greg Tyler were sure to make everything just that much worse.

So she had gone to Provincetown, determined to stay away from men. And she stuck to her guns for an impressive total of three days.

Three days!

Three goddamned days and her legs were as far apart as the North and South Poles again!

Three days!

Still, three days was almost a record for her. And she could have gone longer if Greg hadn't appeared looking like Apollo incarnate.

Damn him, anyway.

Of course he *was* good. Good-looking, but not a washout like so damned many good-looking men. Imaginative, too—and plenty of stamina, which was important. But when you came right down to it, sex was pretty much the same no matter who it was who was doing the boffing. There were variations within variations and variations on top of variations, but all in all it always added up to one thing:

Fun.

And, all in all, it never added up to one other thing:

Satisfaction.

It was fun no matter how you did it. Underneath, on top, sideways—if you happened to be Sheila Paine then you happened to like it no matter whether you were looking at the sky or the ground or off into space.

Sitting down, standing up, bending over.

Fun.

With tall men, with short men, with skinny men, with fat men, with young men, with old men, with white men and brown men and yellow men. A man, after all, was a man, and Sheila Paine, after all, was Sheila Paine, and what more could you say about it?

So you liked it whatever way you did it. Liked it? Hell, you loved it. You needed it the way fish need water, and you lived in it and breathed in it and swam around in it, and you were too much woman for any man in the world to handle.

There was only one sore point.

You never climaxed.

Nymphomaniac.

According to *Webster's New World Dictionary of the American Language*, a nymphomaniac is a woman having nymphomania. Nymphomania, again according to the editors of *Webster's New World Dictionary of the American Language*—who should know better—is excessive and uncontrollable sexual desire in a woman.

That's not quite it.

Nymphomania implies more than that the girl in question is a benefactor of the male sex. Clinically, a nymphomaniac is a woman who does not fully enjoy sex. She is, in a sense, frigid, but she differs from a frigid woman in one important respect.

She *likes* it.

She likes it—but it never turns out to be what she had hoped for at the beginning. She likes it, but she goes through life without an orgasm, hops from bed to bed without ever finding a bed or a bed partner that is truly satisfactory.

And, of course, she keeps hopping from bed to bed. That's where the excessive and uncontrollable sexual desire comes in. The nymphomaniac keeps searching for the perfect man, the man who can satisfy her.

She never finds him.

Sheila Paine was a nymphomaniac. She was twenty-three

years old, and for ten of those twenty-three years she had survived without a hymen.

And without an orgasm.

She was born in Macon, Georgia. She lived there with her family until she was fourteen years old and matured with the rapidity of girls in the southern United States. Her body was a grown-up body when she was eleven years old and a student in the seventh grade at Public School #14. Her breasts were full and ripe and perfect by then, her legs slender without being the least bit scrawny. Her hair, dirty blonde at birth, was already its ash-blonde color by that time and her face was already beautiful, although it didn't then possess the adult beauty that it later developed.

The boys noticed her. When she was twelve, sixteen- and seventeen- and eighteen-year-old boys turned to whistle at her as she walked down the street. Older men took a second look at her even then.

When she was thirteen she stopped being a virgin.

That was the way she thought of it—as if a previous state simply ended. It happened easily enough and it wasn't the traumatic experience it is for so many girls, especially when it happens at so young an age. It was pleasant, as it always was for her in the future, and it was unsatisfying, also as it always was in the future. Very few girls ever reach orgasm the first time, but for Sheila it was the beginning of a pattern.

It happened, strangely enough, in her own home. She was home alone that day. It was summer and school was out, and that year she had decided she was old enough to stay at home instead of going to summer camp as she had done for the past several years. Her father was at work at the mill and her mother was playing canasta at another woman's house.

Sheila was alone.

Martin Crawford was also home in the house next door. He was a big, hulking boy, long on muscles and correspondingly short on brains, a big nineteen-year-old refugee from an Erskine Caldwell novel.

He was in his back yard.

Sheila was in her back yard. She was wearing shorts and a halter and a good deal of Sheila was left uncovered by the combination.

Martin was watering his lawn. When he saw her he stared at her stupidly and almost dropped the hose. His eyes focused first on her prominent breasts that rode high in the skimpy polka-dot halter. Then his eyes went to her already-full hips that bulged against the sides of the matching polka-dot shorts.

His stupid eyes bulged halfway out of their sockets. His stupid tongue dropped halfway out of his mouth. His stupid hands got hot and sweaty and his pulse rate went up, and breathing suddenly became considerably more of a chore than it had been before he looked at her.

"Hey," he said.

She looked at him.

"Hiya, Sheila."

"Hi."

"Whatcha doing?"

"Nothing," she said, which was quite true.

"Can I come over?"

"Sure," she said.

There was a fence between the two yards. It was an easy fence to climb, but for an uncoordinated ass like Martin Crawford it was an insurmountable obstacle. She waited while he walked hurriedly down his driveway, around the front of the house and into her driveway.

"Hiya," he said again.

"Hi."

"Awful hot out," he said.

She agreed.

"Even hotter than it was yesterday, and the paper said it was a record breaker yesterday. Guess that makes it plenty hot."

She caught him looking at her breasts and the thought came to her that she ought to be angry at him. But she wasn't angry. Instead she was rather pleased without knowing quite why his glance pleased her.

"Sure is hot," he offered again.

"My folks have the bedroom air-conditioned," she said.

"Yeah?"

"They just got the air-conditioner a month ago," she said. "Pa says the thing to do is air-condition the house a room at a time. I'll have one next year, and then I guess they'll go on to the downstairs."

Now he was looking at her hips. His gaze was centered upon the spot between her thighs.

"If your folks got the bedroom air-conditioned," he said, "how come you're sitting out here in the yard?"

"I don't know."

"I mean it must be cooler up there."

"It's real cool. Nice and comfortable."

"Then how come you're out here where it's so hot?"

"Just wanted to get some sun."

Martin shifted from one foot to the other. He was nervous.

"Say," he said at length, "maybe we could go up there if it's so nice and cool. Huh?"

"Gee, I don't know."

"I mean it's so dang hot—"

"I don't know. I wanted to get some tan on me."

"You got a pretty fair tan as it is."

"That's the trouble," she said. "It's fair, and I want it tan instead of fair."

"Look," he said. "I mean, we could go upstairs for awhile just to cool off."

"Well—"

"It's awful dang hot."

"All right," she said.

She led him into the house and up the staircase to the second floor. The air-conditioner was running in her parents' room and they closed the door once they were inside so that the room would stay nice and cool.

Thirteen-year-old Sheila Paine kicked off her sandals and curled up girlishly on the big double bed.

Nineteen-year-old Martin Crawford sat awkwardly in a big armchair and stared at her.

"Sure is cool," he said.

She agreed with him, wondering how anybody as old as Martin Crawford could be so godawful stupid.

"You cool?"

She nodded.

"Bet you'd be cooler without that on."

"Without what on?"

He pointed to the polka-dot halter.

"You think so?"

"Yeah."

She looked hard at him and he averted his eyes from hers. He was embarrassed now, afraid he had gone too far.

"I don't believe you, Martin."

He didn't say anything.

"I don't believe you," she repeated. "I think you just want to get a look."

His face turned red.

His mouth dropped open and he began to stammer incoherently. His face was redder than ever.

"I'm not mad," she said. "I'll let you look if you really want to."

"You mean it?"

"Sure."

She removed her halter.

He moved from the chair to the bed, and she decided that it was undoubtedly the fastest Martin Crawford had moved in all the nineteen years he had been alive. He stared at her breasts with fascination.

"Gawd," he said.

His interest was doing things to her. Strange things. And all at once she wanted him to do more than just look.

"You want to touch 'em, Martin?"

He wanted to very much. He touched and stroked her breasts as if they were the most wonderful and unbelievable things in the entire world, and she started squirming on the bed.

Her voice husky, she said: "Maybe I'd be even cooler if I took my shorts off. You think so, Martin?"

He couldn't answer.

She took off the shorts and leaned back against the pillow.

"Touch me," she commanded.

He touched her. It was the strangest and most wonderful feeling she had ever had.

"Martin—"

He looked at her.

"If you took off your clothes I bet you'd be cooler, too."

The idiot blushed.

"Come on," she said. "It's not fair, you getting to look at me and me not getting a chance to look at you."

He took off his clothes and dropped them on the chair. She looked at him with a great deal of interest that she didn't take the trouble to conceal. It was the first time she had ever seen a naked man, and she noted the details with interest and fondled him gently.

She didn't know what was supposed to come next.

He did.

He pushed her back on the bed. His breath was hot in her face and he was sweating like a pig in a furnace.

"Come on," he said.

"What should I do?"

He showed her what to do.

"I won't hurt you," he told her.

But he wasn't telling the truth. He did hurt her, hurt her very badly and painfully, hurt her so much that she felt as though there was a knife inside her that was cutting her and tearing her to ribbons.

She moaned and she cried.

But she loved every minute of it.

Afterwards, when he was gone from the house, some dormant instinct made her change her parents' bed and throw out the bloody sheet so that her mother would not find out what she had done.

But her mother did find out.

Not from the sheet. Sheila had handled that part of it very well.

Martin, however, didn't know enough to keep his big mouth shut.

He told his friends. Since he only had one or two friends in the world, this might not have made much difference. But he also told his acquaintances, and they told their acquaintances, and pretty soon the male population of Macon was aware of the fact that Sheila Paine was no longer a virgin.

Sheila Paine then enjoyed the most incredible rash of popularity that ever visited a thirteen-year-old girl. The telephone at the Paine house rang day and night. Boys were calling her incessantly, dating her incessantly, seeing her incessantly.

And, naturally, loving her incessantly.

And the word spread.

And Sheila's parents knew. They couldn't help knowing.

Her father left his job as a plant manager because of her. They didn't tell her this at the time, but told her instead that he had been promoted to another branch in Lowell, Massachusetts. But the job in Lowell was a voluntary demotion rather than a promotion. He had started in Lowell before Sheila was born. Then the textile company opened up a branch factory in Macon where the workers hadn't yet had the brains to organize themselves into unions. Labor was cheap and the factory did very well.

Now the Paines were on their way back to Lowell. Tom and Lottie Paine didn't much like the idea of heading back north at first—you put down deep roots over a period of fourteen years. But they were basically New Englanders, never thoroughly comfortable in the South, and besides their daughter's comfort and reputation was more important than where they lived.

But their daughter's reputation was no better in Lowell. Sex was still sex and Sheila was still Sheila and boys were still boys. She struggled to stop, but finally she got to the point were the mere touch of a boy's hand on hers was enough to set her off.

She had had over a hundred lovers by the time she was seventeen.

After that she stopped keeping count.

She graduated from high school and went for a year to Boston University. Then she dropped out of school and at the same time cut off all ties with her family, not so much because she didn't love them as because she was disappointing them constantly. She worked in Boston, drifting from one secretarial job to another, getting an occasional check from home, living inexpensively and going to bed with just about everybody who came along.

Once she went to a psychiatrist.

She wound up making love with him on the couch in his office, and she never went back to him again.

CHAPTER 4

Madelaine hesitated outside the house. It was a white frame building on Winthrop Street, a two-story saltbox affair with forbidding brown shutters and matching brown trim. The door was open and music mingled with laughter and animated conversation within the house.

The Hookery.

"Don't miss the parties at the Hookery," the girls had told her. "They aren't gay sets, not exactly. But every Friday night they have a big mixer open to anybody who wants to come. Men pay a buck a head and gals go free. All the wine you want and a little food to soak up the wine with. Music and dancing—and you can't miss running into at least a couple of gay girls there. Nice ones, too—not the truck driver types you'll find at the Old Barn and the other gay bars."

That's what the girls had said.

So here she was on Winthrop Street standing in front of the Hookery and getting up the courage to go inside. Bruce Ryerson, the clod who tried to pick her up in the Purple Oyster, had almost succeeded in convincing her to stay away from the party that night. He had invited her to go with him, or at least he had been about to invite her, and an invitation from Bruce Ryerson ordinarily would have been enough to scare her away.

But at the last minute she had decided to give the party a try. After the reception she had given Bruce Ryerson that afternoon she seriously doubted that he would prove to be much of a nuisance to her. He would probably look the other way if he saw her approaching, and that was fine with her. Why should she pass up a party just because some clod couldn't look at her without getting filthy ideas?

Besides, she admitted to herself, she felt like a party that night. She was lonely, annoyingly lonely. She wanted two things—the company of happy people in a happy room and the chance to meet a girl who would love her and whom she would love.

She had dressed for the party. Fortunately the night was cool enough so that she had the chance to wear the kind of outfit she looked best in without making herself uncomfortable. She wore a tight-fitting jersey dress that was as black as her hair and it hugged her slender body like a lover. A girl who was bigger in the hips and breasts couldn't wear a dress like that without looking almost cheap, but Madelaine was small and slim enough to carry it off. She looked lovely, and she knew very well that she looked lovely.

She took a deep breath and marched up the steps to the door of the Hookery. The boy at the door let her pass through and another boy handed her a glass of sweet red wine. She walked slowly into the crowded room and found a seat on the end of a couch along one wall.

The Hookery was sort of an indoor cave. There were about thirty people all told sitting on the couch or on the rug or, as sort of a compromise between the two, on little pillows on the floor.

In the far corner of the room a boy was playing a guitar and half a dozen people were singing "Blow The Candles Out."

> *Your mother and your father*
> *In yonder room do lie*
> *Enjoying one another*
> *So why not you and I?*
>
> *Enjoying one another*
> *With ne'er a care or doubt*
> *So roll me in your arms, love*
> *And blow the candles out!*

It was fortunate, Madelaine reflected, that none of them followed the advice of the song. A dozen-odd candles stuck in empty chianti bottles provided the sole illumination in the huge room. The windows were all opened wide and the candles flickered in a gentle but persistent breeze.

She sipped her wine.

The wine was good, and when she finished the glass she went back to the boy with the bottle and got a refill. On the way she spotted Bruce Ryerson, his hand not-too-subtly rubbing a girl's thigh and his eyes staring soulfully into the eyes of the girl. But the sight of him didn't upset her at all, to her surprise. The wine was good and she could already feel the effects of it; the party was good and she was enjoying herself.

Seated once again on the corner of the couch, she remembered why she had come to the party in the first place. She needed a woman, needed one desperately, and as she thought about her need she grew passionate at once, hot and hungry for a woman.

She scanned the room, hoping that there was another gay girl present. After a few years in the world of lesbianism a girl could develop a sort of sixth sense that enabled her to recognize a sister in the middle of a crowd or across a crowded room. The sixth sense wasn't infallible but it worked a good deal of the time. It had to—otherwise life and love became a good deal more difficult.

Her eyes looked over the room. A girl here and there seemed a remote possibility—not a sure thing, but worth reconnaissance if nothing else turned up. But in each case the girl was not particularly attractive to Madelaine.

She kept looking.

Then her eyes lit on the big blonde and she fell instantly and completely in love.

The girl with the short brown hair took Bruce Ryerson's hand from her thigh and placed it back in his lap. He returned it to her thigh and gave her a squeeze. She picked up the hand a second time and dropped it in his lap.

"You're working awfully fast, aren't you?"

He grinned at her. He put his hand on her thigh again.

This time she didn't remove it.

"I always work fast," he said, "when there's something as nice as you to work with."

She looked down at his hand. Then she crossed her legs neatly so that the hand wound up in midair with no thigh under it. He gave up and grinned at her again.

"I'd better tell you right now," she said. "I'm not that kind of a girl."

"What kind?"

"The kind you think I am."

"Oh? What kind do I think you are?"

She didn't return his grin but looked down at the floor instead.

"The kind you can sleep with the first time you see her."

"Hell," he said, "I didn't even ask you yet. You could at least wait until you're asked."

"I—"

"What kind of a girl *are* you, anyway?"

He was teasing her and she knew it, but she didn't respond like a person being teased. She wanted to be serious, and all he seemed to be interested in was a quick pick-up and a quick feel and a quick trip to a bedroom for a quick tumble on a bed. That wasn't what she wanted.

"I'm a schoolteacher," she said. "A fourth-grade teacher on summer vacation."

"Oh," he said.

"That doesn't mean I'm a frigid virgin," she said seriously. "It doesn't mean I'm just interested in sex either."

"I see," he said, looking into her eyes now and matching her seriousness with a vaguely serious expression of his own. He could make her, he decided, could make her without too much effort at all. But the enthusiasm of the chase was beginning to leave him. Hell, the little iceberg probably wasn't worth the trouble to bang her anyway. She was pretty in a quiet sort of a way and he knew that her legs and breasts were nice enough, but he preferred a babe with a little more flair.

He looked around the room while the schoolteacher went on talking about something. He nodded, pretending to listen. Actually he was busy looking over the other women at the party.

His eyes landed on the girl he had seen in the Purple Oyster, the girl who put him down so hard he was still shaky. Man, some day he'd have to get next to a piece like that! But tonight wasn't the night to try for her. Tonight he wanted a sure thing.

Something like that big blonde, he thought. She was with a guy now, but it shouldn't be too hard to get her away from him. And she looked like she'd be worth it. A body like hers would really be something to ride around on.

He licked his lips in anticipation.

Then he turned back to the schoolteacher, smiling warmly into her eyes and wondering how long it would be before he got rid of her.

Greg Tyler was sitting in an armchair. Sheila was on his lap, a full glass of wine in her hand. She drank half the wine in one swallow.

It was her third glass.

"I don't know why in hell we had to come here," she said.

"It's a party."

"So what? We could have had our own party."

He looked at her. She cuddled closer to him and her lips were inches away from his neck. She pressed her lips against his neck and bit him gently.

He wished she could be a little less demonstrative. Hell, he was hardly a cold person, but there were a good thirty people in the room and she didn't have to crawl all over him with all of them watching. Even the bit on the beach, wonderful and satisfying as it had been, was a little too public for his taste.

Sex was something private—something that had to mean something to the people involved in it if it was going to be much good. If it was just the useless, purposeless copulation of animals, it was a waste of time. And he was beginning to think that all Sheila was interested in was sex. Twice in her cottage when he had picked her up, twice earlier on the beach—maybe she didn't get tired of it, but he sure as hell did. And it wasn't as though he wasn't in shape for it. He could handle just about any woman, but he was beginning to wonder if Sheila was worth handling.

She drank the rest of her wine in another swallow and went off to fill the glass again. That was another thing, he thought. She was going to be looped if she kept drinking the way she had been so far. And God only knew what she would be like when she had a load on. Maybe it wouldn't be a bad idea to get away from her before then.

Sheila, he decided, was the perfect woman to meet when you were seventeen or eighteen years old. Then all the sex was a perfectly delightful enterprise. A few years later you'd had as many girls as you wanted and there had to be more to it than pure sex to keep you interested for any length of time.

He would leave her before the night was over. He didn't want her any more and he knew she could find somebody else without any trouble. There were a good many more men than women at the party to begin with, and a girl who looked like Sheila could get a man without half trying.

And any man, he knew, would do. He was just a man to her, and he had the feeling that no other qualifications were necessary if you wanted to play games with a girl like Sheila Paine.

Sheila filled the glass with wine and emptied it without putting the bottle back on the table. Her head was swimming nicely now.

In the corner they were singing:

> *Mama, mama—take a look at sis*
> *Mama, mama—take a look at sis*
> *Come on, Mama, take a look at sis*
> *Up upon the levee doin' a double twist—*
> *Whining boy*
> *Don't forget my name . . .*

Sheila refilled her glass.

It was bad, she thought. Very bad and getting worse. The party was so nice and she felt so good that she knew something perfectly horrible was going to happen. She could feel the strains and tensions building up within her mind and body until she wanted to take off her clothes and lie down on the floor and scream her head off.

Instead she drank some more wine.

Very bad, she thought. If Greg was a gentleman they wouldn't be at the party now. They would be back at her shack making the bedsprings whine.

And in the corner they were singing:

> *Sister, sister—dirty little sow*
> *Sister, sister—dirty little sow*
> *Sister, sister, you're a dirty sow*
> *You wanna be a bad girl but you don't know how—*
> *Whining boy*
> *Don't forget my name . . .*

There was a hand on her elbow and Sheila turned around, her legs just the least bit unsteady. The girl standing in front of her was a head shorter than she was and very pretty, with black hair and a slender body encased in a tight black knit dress.

The girl was Madelaine Carr.

"Hello," the girl said.

"Hello."

"My name is Madelaine," the girl said. "Madelaine Carr."

"Sheila Paine."

"This is a nice party, isn't it?"

"Very nice," Sheila said, wondering vaguely what the point of the question was.

"A very gay party."

"I suppose so," Sheila said. There seemed to be some hidden meaning in the girl's remark, some extra message in the way the pretty little thing was looking up at her. But she couldn't figure out what it was.

"I'll see you," the girl said. She seemed sad and she turned and walked back to where she had been sitting.

And in the corner they were singing:

> *Woke up in the morning*
> *Feeling mighty bad*
> *Wanted to make it with my mother*
> *And kill my dad—*
> *I got those mean and evil*
> *Oedipal fixation blues . . .*

"Greg."

She was sitting in his lap now. Her arms were around his neck, and while she knew that he didn't like what she was doing she also knew that she couldn't help herself.

"Greg, let's get out of here."

"Where do you want to go?"

"They've got a bedroom in the back," she said. "Let's use it."

"Stop it," he said. He took her hands from behind his neck and put them back in her lap.

She pouted.

"Sheila—"

"Come on," she said. "I want to go to the bedroom."

"Sheila—" His voice had an edge to it this time.

Louder she said: "I want to go to the bedroom, damn you!"

The room quieted down. People were beginning to look at them.

"Sheila, if you can't behave—"

"Behave?" She was shouting now.

"Yes, behave."

"Who in hell wants to behave? I don't want to behave. I want to get fixed. What the hell do you think I came here for?"

He slapped her.

She stood up, her hand flying to her face where her cheek was red from the slap. The blow was all she had needed. Now any last vestige of inhibition was gone and she was nothing but a sex-hungry animal who had to be taken quickly before she went out of her mind.

"*You bastard!*"

He stood up, too. His face was white with fury and he wanted only to get away from her, far away from her.

"I'm going," he said, his voice thin with rage.

"So go! What do I care?"

"Good-bye," he told her, turning away from her. "You can find somebody else to take you home."

"Go to hell," she shouted after him. "You think you're the only man in the goddamned world? I'll find somebody who can give me what I'm looking for, damn you. I'll find somebody who wants to go to the bedroom!"

Across the room Bruce Ryerson detached himself from the schoolteacher and stood up, smiling down at the girl.

"You'll have to excuse me," he said. "I think I'm being paged."

Madelaine Carr walked alone. The night was black around her and there were neither stars nor a moon in the dark sky. She was almost invisible—a dark-haired girl in a black dress walking alone on an unlit street under a starless and moonless sky.

Maybe it was better to be invisible.

Evidently she had made a mistake about that girl, that big and blonde and strikingly beautiful girl, that Sheila Paine. She certainly muffed every cue Madelaine handed her, and for awhile there Madelaine had been handing her cues on a silver platter.

God, she was beautiful.

But she couldn't have Sheila Paine, that was obvious. It was also obvious that somebody else was going to have Sheila Paine within a minute or two—the girl was practically climbing the walls, she was so hot for a man. And this severely limited the pleasure of the party at the Hookery as far as Madelaine was concerned.

Now she had to find a woman. Had to find one fast, very fast, before she herself was climbing the walls in frustration. She had to find a woman, and she was going to the place women always went when they had to find other women in a hurry.

She was going to a gay bar.

The bar was the Old Barn and the girls in Boston had had unpleasant things to say about it. She'd probably wind up with a butch, according to all available reports, and she didn't like butches. Mannish women dressed in pants, truck driver types with ducktail haircuts and swear words spilling from their lips.

But beggars could not be choosers.

She hurried along in the direction of the Old Barn.

Greg pushed his way through the mob of people to the door. He couldn't take the place another minute and he wanted only to get out and get some air.

"Wait a minute," a voice said.

It was the schoolteacher. She followed him outside and they stood together on the sidewalk, looking at each other awkwardly. She was quite attractive, Greg realized—pretty, while not being nearly so dynamically attractive as Sheila was. This girl was pretty in a quiet sort of way.

"I couldn't take any more of that," the girl was saying.

"Neither could I."

"If that's their idea of a party—"

"They can keep it," he finished for her.

They stood looking at each other. He shifted his weight from one foot to the other, wondering idly what her game was.

"Look," she said suddenly. "I have to tell you something."

He waited for her to go ahead.

"I'm a schoolteacher," she said. "I have a fourth grade class back in Pawtucket and I teach them things. That's what I do ten months of the year."

He nodded, listening.

"I'm here for the summer," she said. "I came here to . . . to meet somebody. Somebody nice."

She was having a great deal of difficulty getting the words out.

"I . . . I want to find somebody to . . . to be with for the summer. Just to be with—do you understand? Somebody to talk to and eat dinner with and go swimming with. Somebody to know and understand—am I making any sense?"

He nodded slowly.

"Somebody to sleep with," she said. "But not until I'm ready to and not for awhile because I've only slept with one man in my whole life and I happen to be scared stiff and besides if it's nothing but sex I just don't want it and—"

He caught her before she could fall. He held her close until he was sure that she wasn't going to cry. Then he released her and took her arm in his.

"Come on," he said softly. "Let's get to know each other."

Sheila was standing up and weaving slightly. She knew dimly what she was doing but she no longer cared about anything but one important thing.

There was a cluster of men around her.

"I'll take you all," she was shouting. "One after the other, goddammit! *One after the other!*"

The men stared at her.

"Never heard of that?" she demanded drunkenly. "They call it a line-up, you morons. Sometimes they call it a gang bang or a midnight review. It's a lot of fun, you idiots!"

A hand caught her around the waist.

"You can come first," she told the owner of the hand. "The rest of you wait your turns. And don't worry because there's plenty here for everybody. You can have seconds or thirds if you're man enough."

She led Bruce Ryerson to the bedroom.

And in the corner they were singing:

> *Keep on trucking, mama*
> *Trucking my blues away*

Keep on trucking, mama
Trucking my blues away
You can do what you do and say what you say
But you better keep going till the break of day—
Keep on trucking, mama
Trucking my blues away . . .

CHAPTER 5

The bedroom was a small room at the rear of the Hookery. An old-fashioned four-poster bed dominated the tiny room and was obviously the center of attraction. This room, like the main room, was illuminated only by candle light. There had been a light switch on the wall near the door but the owners had removed it.

Sheila was in a hurry. She whipped off her blouse and hurled it into one corner of the room. Her hands were trembling with desire and anticipation as she stepped out of her skirt. First her bra and then her panties followed the skirt into the corner of the room.

Bruce Ryerson was having trouble getting out of his clothing. He was excited, more excited than he could remember being, and his hands were clumsy as he unbuttoned and discarded his shirt and unbelted and unzipped and discarded his pants.

Then he was naked, too.

Naked and ready for her.

"Come *on!*"

He wished it would last forever.

It didn't.

He rolled away from her, exhausted, used up, feeling ready for the ashcan. He reached out a hand to touch her breasts but she brushed it away impatiently.

"For a guy who was so anxious," she said evenly, "you sure as hell got done in a hurry."

Next and next and next. Sheila felt like an adding machine whose keys were being danced upon by the cloven hooves of the Great God Pan.

An IBM machine.

A Univac.

Automation.

Food and sex are Nature's basic hungers. Millions of Americans were eating themselves to death. Millions more were killing themselves on the divan of love. Hear the clickety-clack of the counting machines.

Listen!

The Old Barn was an old barn.

That's how it seemed to Madelaine. It had been aptly named; from the Dutch roof to the huge door the building looked more like a barn than most barns did. She had the feeling, looking at the front of the large red building, that it would probably smell like a barn as well.

She walked through the wide doorway, fully expecting the odor of manure to hit her in the face.

While the Old Barn didn't smell like a barn, it was as unpleasant inside as it would have been if it were covered from wall to wall with horse manure. A long brown bar ran the length of the place and women who didn't look much like women lined the bar and drank their liquor neat. There were a few tables with red-and-white checkered table cloths. The entire floor, even the small area set aside for dancing purposes, was completely covered with sawdust. Madelaine supposed that the sawdust was designed to lend a feeling of rustic atmosphere to the place.

She decided that the effort was wasted.

As soon as she walked in she felt eyes upon her, hard eyes, mannish eyes. She had never been able to enjoy the way a real butch sized up a prospective "femme." They were, in her opinion, the next thing to men—and she didn't want men.

She wanted women.

But beggars could not be choosers.

She started walking to the bar, knowing that she wouldn't get there without being approached. And she was right—she had taken just three steps before a tall butch wearing tight dungarees and a black leather jacket and looking for all the world like Hollywood's notion of the contemporary American male juvenile delinquent appeared magically before her, hands on hips and leer on lips. Dark brown hair combed into a rough-looking ducktail haircut and slicked down with plenty of grease, broad shoulders and a narrow waist—she looked as though she had been stamped from a mold.

"Hi, doll," said the butch.

"Hello."

"My name's Mitch—Brenda Mitchell, but they call me Mitch."

"Madelaine Carr."

"Don't think I've seen you around this craphole before, Madelaine."

"I've never been here before."

"Where *have* you been, baby?"

"Sylvia's," Madelaine answered, naming a popular gay bar in Boston. She had only been to Sylvia's twice and had hated it on each occasion, but it was a good name to drop.

"Yeah?"

She nodded.

"I like you," Mitch said. "C'mon and I'll buy you a drink."

Madelaine didn't want a drink.

Madelaine didn't like Mitch.

But she let Mitch buy her the drink.

"Do you want another drink, Maddy?"

She shook her head. She didn't want another drink and she didn't want to stay around the Old Barn any longer. Even though she found Mitch relatively unappealing at first, Mitch was a woman, an available woman.

And now she wanted Mitch so badly she could hardly remain on her feet.

"Let's get out of here," she whispered.

Mitch understood. She took Madelaine's arm and tucked it under her own. Then she led the smaller girl to the door and out into the cool night air.

"You're beautiful," Mitch told her.

"Thank you."

"Real beautiful. You got a place we can go to?"

Madelaine closed her eyes and got a vivid mental picture of the expression on her landlady's face if she should happen to walk up the stairs of her rooming house on the arm of a butch like Mitch.

"No," she said. "I haven't got a place."

"That's okay. We can go to my pad."

Mitch had a car, a two-tone green Chevy coupe. She sat close to Mitch on the front seat while the butch started up the car and drove to the cottage where she lived.

It was a small cottage, clean and neat and relatively modern. Mitch kept the place like a man accustomed to bachelor living—neat and clean, everything in its proper place, but with none of the feminine qualities present in a real woman's living quarters.

They went at once to the bedroom. Mitch caught Madelaine up in her arms and kissed her hard—too hard, and Madelaine's lips were bruised by the kiss.

But it sent her pulse racing.

Mitch's hand on her breast through the jersey dress sent her heart beating still faster and she had to lean on Mitch in order to remain standing.

She couldn't wait. She stepped back and started to pull the tight dress over her head.

"Hang on," Mitch said. "Let me do that for you."

She was very solicitous. She had undressed Madelaine very carefully and deliberately; then she had taken off her own clothes and pressed the smaller girl against her, a soft small body against a big hard body, and the fires burned within Madelaine.

Mitch drew back the bed clothing. Madelaine stretched out on top of the sheet and lay very limp, open and defenseless.

"Please," she whimpered.

"What's the matter, baby?"

"Please hurry, Mitch."

Then Mitch was holding her in her strong arms, kissing her passionately.

"Now," she said softly. The word was less than a whisper and she was saying it more to herself than to Mitch. But Mitch heard her and Mitch understood her. Mitch would have liked to go more slowly and to take more time, but at that particular moment Mitch loved Madelaine very much.

So she played it Madelaine's way.

A rush of magnificent sensation overwhelmed Madelaine. It was beginning now, beginning, and it was perfect, absolutely perfect, and she loved it, loved it so much, loved it and loved it and loved it and loved it and she was burning, burning and steaming and going absolutely out of her mind.

"*How?*"

"Come on," Number Twelve said. "I'll show you."

Number Twelve was not a big man. He was about five and a half feet tall, wiry rather than heavily muscled, with dark wavy hair and a craggy face. He was about thirty-eight years old.

He showed her.

"Like it?"

"Yeah."

"How can you keep this up?"

"Shut up."

He shut up.

He started to pull his clothes on.

"Through already?"

Number Twelve looked at her wonderingly.

"Wanna know what?" Number Twelve said.

"What?"

"You're sick." Number Twelve went on. "You're the sickest I ever saw. And I've seen sick ones."

"Who asked you," Sheila said. "Did you come in here for a good time or a lecture?"

He shook his head as he left.

"Send in number thirteen," Sheila said.

Madelaine's eyes were closed. Mitch lay on the bed beside her, her eyes also closed, her face relaxed in the peace of deep sleep.

Madelaine couldn't sleep.

She was rested, completely rested, rested in a way that she had not been in days. Her whole body was relaxed and the inferno in her loins had been doused in the ideal manner. By all rules she should have been asleep by this time.

But she wasn't.

She opened her eyes but there was nothing to see. The room was completely dark and she could barely make out the sleeping form of Mitch at her side. Tentatively she reached out a hand to touch Mitch but restrained herself before there was any contact between the two of them. Her hand dropped back to her side and stayed there.

She felt rotten.

It wasn't Mitch's fault. In fact, it was quite the opposite. She had come prepared to hate and despise the butch. She had made satisfying and efficient use of the masculine girl—and now she couldn't help feeling guilty for exploiting her.

Mitch had been good—good *to* her and good *for* her. Mitch had been kind and good and sweet and undemanding and totally unselfish—and all the while she felt nothing for Mitch, nothing but slight compassion and a trace of disgust.

While she had been busy using Mitch, Mitch in turn had been busy loving her.

It wasn't fair.

Mitch was a person, a warm person and a good person. If some of the butch's mannerisms and affectations repelled Madelaine, that was probably just repression on her part, a reaction attributable to her own lesbianism. Mitch was different, naturally. But she herself was certainly a deviate from the norm and as warped in her own way as Mitch, if not more so.

Mitch loved her.

And all she felt for Mitch was compassion.

It wasn't fair at all.

She rolled over on her side away from the butch, her eyes open once again looking out of the window into the blackness of the night. It would be good if only she could let herself love Mitch. The summer would fly and everything would be very beautiful and wonderful.

If only she could love Mitch.

But she couldn't. She couldn't possibly love Mitch because she was in love with somebody else, somebody whom she loved with an unbelievably strong love, somebody whose face had floated through her mind all the while that Mitch was making love to her.

Somebody with blonde hair. Ash-blonde hair.

Somebody with huge breasts and rolling hips.

Somebody who was tall, tall and magnificent.

Somebody who was *not* gay, not gay at all. Somebody, in fact, who was at the very opposite end of the line.

Somebody who would probably never be the least bit interested in Madelaine Carr.

Somebody named Sheila Paine.

Madelaine got up from the bed. Her knees were weak and she could hardly stand, but she dressed quickly and silently, being very careful not to rouse Mitch from her sleep. She couldn't sleep there, not with Mitch asleep at her side, and she didn't want to wake up the following morning in Mitch's bed with Mitch beside her. It wasn't fair to the other girl and it would not be pleasant either.

Dressing was not difficult. She had worn only a pair of black panties beneath the dress—a bra was unnecessary, both because of the dress itself and because her little breasts were more than firm enough to get along without being stuffed into a brassiere.

She put on her panties and her dress and her shoes. She walked on tiptoe to the door and opened it noiselessly. She turned, and something inside her made her blow a silent kiss at the sleeping form of Mitch.

Then she left the cottage.

It was a long way back to her own rooming-house but she

didn't mind the walk. She covered the ground very swiftly, her mind in a whirl and her feet walking automatically, first one and then the other.

When she was snug in her own bed with her clothes off again and the white linen sheet covering her to her neck, the mental tensions evaporated just as the physical ones had given way to Mitch's insistent hands and mouth. Her head spun around dizzily for a moment or two.

Then sleep came and everything was good again.

Sheila was about to be sick.

Her stomach was making weird motions within her and she realized that it was about to expel its contents. With a tremendous effort she rushed to the window and yanked it open, getting it open just in time.

Then she let go of everything that was creating such a ruckus in her poor stomach.

Opening the window had been a waste of time.

There was a screen on the window.

When she realized this she burst into laughter. Somehow it seemed to sum up everything. She laughed and laughed and barely managed to make her way to the door.

She opened the door.

"Next!"

But there was nobody left.

Now she couldn't hold herself together any longer. Everything gave way at once. Her mind went completely blank and her knees turned to rubber. She reached out with one hand to clutch at the doorjamb but her fingers refused to do what her mind was unable to dictate. Her fingers brushed the doorjamb and she crumpled to the floor.

She was unconscious before she hit the floor. She lay in the doorway like a lump of battered clay—naked and bruised, worn out and completely exhausted.

She couldn't have moved if they burned the building down around her.

Chapter 6

She was conscious of the music before she was aware of anything else. Her eyes were still closed, her muscles still relaxed, her body still motionless under the covers. She didn't know who she was or where she was or what in the world she was doing wherever and whoever she was, but she did know that there was music playing.

So she listened to the music.

She liked it, and she tried to remember if she had ever heard it before. It sounded remotely familiar but she couldn't place it or be sure who it was who had written it. The piece that was playing was a string quartet with a clarinet going in the background. It sounded vaguely Haydnish or Mozarty but she wasn't sure what it was.

She remained under the covers, remained motionless and silent and kept her eyes tightly closed. Now she knew that she was Sheila Paine, but she still couldn't figure out where she was.

Well, wherever she was, how had she gotten there?

Let's see . . . she was on the beach and a man came along and wham bam. Then she was in her cottage and the man came to see her again and wham bam. Then the man took her to a party and then the man walked out on her.

And then—

Oh. With a sickening flood of nausea she remembered. All the events of the previous evening suddenly paraded before her closed eyes and her stomach started to turn over on its ear and her brain swam around in a world of sea-green mucous. All the wine, all the words, and all the men. All the horrible, terrible, sickening, nauseating, stomach-churning men and all the terrible things they had done to her.

Sheila Paine.

Sheila Paine—gang bang girl.

The facts were bad enough. It was certainly terrible enough that she had done what she had, but it was much worse that she had to remember about it the next day. Other people seemed to black out when they had a lot of alcohol—they never remembered the next morning what they had done the night before. They got headaches and thirsts and hangovers, but they never remembered.

She, on the other hand, never got a hangover. Even now her head was clear and her throat no drier than normal.

But she never forgot.

She relaxed again for a moment and let herself tune in on the music again. Well, it was a string quartet by somebody with a clarinet thrown in. Maybe she could get up and find out who it was by, and at the same time she could find out why she was where she was and all that. She knew without looking that she was not at her own little hovel in the woods. For one thing, she didn't have a record player. For another, the bed she was lying on didn't possess the old familiar sag of the bed in her cottage.

But getting up and looking didn't seem to be worth the effort. It was much easier to stay put. It was much easier to remain wherever she was and let the music wash over her with warm soothing waves. To hell with the rest of the world. To hell with all the men in it. To hell with everybody, up to and including Sheila Paine.

She listened to the music. The clarinet seemed to soar over the heads of the violins and viola and cello, reaching newer and greater heights and striving toward a momentous orchestral orgasm. She found herself hoping the clarinet would make it.

Somebody had to, for God's sake.

She almost giggled at that. She suppressed the giggle, however, and snuggled closer to the pillow that nestled against her cheek. Then, suddenly, a thought came to her.

How did she know she was alone?

Well, what did it matter?

But the thought nagged at her and finally made her sit up in the bed. She was sitting straight up with her hands clutching the sheet up above her breasts before she opened her eyes. At last she opened them and blinked at the light of the day, her eyes wide.

The man said: "Hello."

"Hello," she answered, since it seemed as though it was the obvious reply. Hell, if somebody says *hello* to you you say *hello* back to him. They taught you that much in kindergarten.

"Did you sleep well?"

"Very well," she said, wondering hysterically who the man was. He looked vaguely familiar but she was almost certain that he hadn't been one of her lovers of the night before. There were so many of them that it was hard to keep them all straight, but it still seemed to her that he hadn't been one of them.

He was dark and slender. His hair was long and black and he

had combed it back neatly. He was young—21 or 22, she guessed, younger than she herself was—and he was quite attractive in a young and sensitive sort of a way. And very familiar.

Where had she seen him before?

He seemed to be waiting for her to say something, so she said the first thing that happened to come to mind.

"What's the music?"

He looked blank for a minute; evidently he hadn't exactly been expecting the question. Then he told her that it was the Mozart Quintet for Clarinet with Reginald Kell and the Budapest String Quartet.

"I think I've heard it before," she told him.

He nodded.

"I guess I made something of a spectacle of myself last night," she said, grossly understating the case.

He looked embarrassed.

"Look," she said, "don't worry about talking about it. I'm not . . . not a very good girl, you might say. This sort of thing has happened before. When I have too much to drink I just let go and nearly anything can happen. Was I bad?"

"Pretty bad," he admitted.

"Did I break up the party?"

"You *were* the party."

"I see," she said. "That's how it usually turns out. It's a hell of a thing, I guess."

He didn't say anything.

"Do you know who I am?"

"You're Sheila Paine, aren't you?"

"That's right. And do you know where I am?"

He didn't seem to understand.

"Look," she said, "it's very simple, really. I know that I'm Sheila Paine, but I'll be damned if I know who you are or where I am or much of anything. Do you see what I'm getting at? Where *are* we?"

Light dawned in his eyes. "Oh," he said. "Gee, I'm sorry. You passed out at the Hookery and they closed the place so I brought you here. This is my cottage—I hope you don't mind."

"Not at all," she said. "I'm very grateful."

"We're just a little ways from downtown P-town," he went on. "If I had known where you lived I would have taken you home, but you were out like a light and I couldn't get you to tell me."

"That's all right," she said. "But you still haven't answered my question."

"Question?"

"Question," she repeated.

"What question?"

"My question," she said. "Who are *you*?"

"Oh," he said. "I see."

"Well?"

"My name is Harvey Chase."

"Hello, Harvey."

"Hello. I run the Purple Oyster."

"What's the Purple Oyster?"

"It's sort of a café," he explained. "We sell coffee and sandwiches and cold drinks, and sometimes people come in and sit and sing a few songs or something like that. Every morning a guy does a little portrait work out front and at night there's a fellow with a guitar who plays. He was the guy playing guitar at the Hookery last night."

"And you run the Purple Oyster?"

"That's right," he said.

"Do you manage it for somebody or what?"

"No, it's my place—I don't own the building because it's cheaper renting, but I lay out the money and take in whatever profits there are."

"You're pretty young for a job like that."

"Twenty-one."

"How come you're not going to college?"

"I finished at Rhode Island a year ago in June."

"Honestly?"

He nodded. "I got through in three years."

"And now you're running the . . . the Purple Oyster?"

"That's right," he said. "I majored in English at Rhode Island and with an English major there's not much you can do outside of teach and I didn't want to wind up teaching. I figure a person who wants to go into teaching ought to, but a person who's just interested in reading is wasting his own time and the time of his students if he becomes a professor. It's not for me."

"I agree with you." She wasn't sure whether or not she agreed with him, and all in all she didn't much care one way or the other. But he was a nice kid, a cute kid, and she just wanted to let him go on talking.

"So I came out to the Cape on vacation last summer and I saw a hole in the wall for rent downtown. I had a little money saved, enough to get started on, and I opened the café figuring it would give me enough money to live on and enough time to take things easy."

"How is it working out?"

"Pretty well," he said. "I'm not making a fortune but I'm getting enough to eat and I'm not killing myself with work. It was rough going the first few months, but even during the winter I was coming close to meeting expenses and this summer I'm in the black."

"How in the world did you know what to do? You didn't have any experience in the business, did you?"

"None at all," he said. "But with a coffee shop you don't need much know how. We don't do any cooking—just drinks and prepared sandwiches. So there's not much you have to know on the technical side of things."

He was far more relaxed now that she had gotten him to talk. She could see this from the way the little lines were gone from around the corners of his mouth, the way his body seemed more at ease in the chair.

"It's a good life," he was saying. "I like to spend a lot of time doing nothing—sitting on a beach, walking by myself, listening to music or reading. This way I have a chance to do these things—I can close the Oyster if I really feel in the mood. And there's nobody who's my boss—that makes a real difference."

He said all this very seriously. Then his mood changed and he seemed to open up. "Enough about me," he said lightly. "Let's talk about you."

•   •   •

So Sheila Paine talked about herself. For once she really felt like opening up about herself. Maybe it was because of the general trauma of the night before, maybe it was just because Harvey Chase was so easy going and young and easy to talk to, but whatever it was she found herself telling him everything there was to tell about her.

She skipped over the surface stuff—where she was from, how old she was, the rest of the trivia. The thing of paramount importance to her was sex, and her sex life occupied the major part of her conversation.

She didn't mince words. She told him about Martin Crawford and the other boys after him. She told him about the way she couldn't help herself, and at the same time about the way she was never satisfied. She knew who and what she was and she had done a good deal of reading on the subject, so she was not talking like a naive schoolgirl who didn't know what was coming off.

He listened to her silently, nodding from time to time, interjecting a *yes* or an *uh-huh* when the conversation called for it. Watching him, she felt that he neither condemned nor failed to sympathize with her. He took everything in and nothing showed on his face, but she decided that she liked him very much.

It was a long time before she finished speaking.

"Now you know all there is to know about me," she said at last. "Now tell me about us."

"Us?"

"Us," she said. "What did we do last night?"

"We didn't do anything."

"Honestly?"

"Honestly."

"Didn't you make love to me?"

"No," he said. "I didn't."

"How come?"

He shrugged.

She frowned suddenly and said: "Maybe the line was too damned long."

He didn't say anything.

"Were you there at the party from the start?"

"Yes."

"Were you with anybody?"

"No—I came by myself."

She sat up straight in the bed, holding the sheet in front of her. She wasn't wearing anything beneath the sheet. She pulled the sheet tighter against herself so that he couldn't help seeing the contour of her breasts.

"How come you didn't make love to me?"

"I don't know."

"Don't you find me attractive?"

He said: "I think you're the most beautiful woman I've ever seen in my life."

"Then . . . say, where did you sleep?"

"On the floor."

She gaped. "The floor? Why didn't you join me in the bed? It's not as if I would have got up screaming if there was a man in bed with me. I'm fairly used to it, you know."

"I—"

He was staring at her and she returned the stare. All at once it seemed to her that she had to have Harvey Chase, and to get him into the bed and had to make love with him. That one goal was all of a sudden very important.

She let go of the sheet.

She was naked to the waist, naked and beautiful. Sunlight that poured through the open window was bright upon her breasts. He tried to avert his eyes from her but he couldn't help looking at her.

"Do you like the way I look?"

"Yes," he said. "You know that I do."

"Do you want to make love to me?"

"More than I've ever wanted anything in my life."

"Then—"

His eyes stared hopelessly into hers. "Sheila," he said, there's something I have to explain to you. I don't know quite how to say it—"

She waited, wondering.

"I've always been sort of . . . well, bookish. I spent most of my time alone from the time I was six or seven years old. In high school I didn't have dates except for the big dances and in college—well, I was all hepped up on the idea of getting out in three years. I spent just about all of my time studying."

"Go on," she said gently.

"What happened," he said, "is that . . . well, nothing happened. I studied and I sat and I read and I never . . . never made love to a girl in my life. Sheila, I'm twenty-one years old and I'm still a virgin!"

•   •   •

"Harvey—"

He was as red as a beet.

"Come here, Harvey. Sit next to me."

He sat beside her on the bed. He was fully dressed; she was bare to the waist and stark naked beneath the thin covering of the sheet.

"Harvey, kiss me."

He kissed her. It was awkward, but he made up in enthusiasm what he lacked in raw talent. She had to teach him to open his mouth when he kissed, had to tease him with her own tongue into moving his tongue in the most exciting and stimulating manner. But he was a good pupil and he seemed to be learning quickly and easily.

Clumsily his hand reached for her breast and held it gently. His touch was awkward but she found it somehow more exciting than the confident caresses of more experienced men. Her desire for Harvey was mixed in equal parts with sympathy and under-standing, and the three ingredients intensified each other. She wanted him, but not with the feverish hunger that was character-istic of her sexual experiences. She wanted everything to be slow and gentle this time.

She was the aggressor now, he the inexperienced and passive one. She unbuttoned the buttons of his plaid shirt and helped him off with it. With practiced fingers she fondled the dark hair on his chest, rubbed his neck and stroked his pale lips.

"Sheila—"

She helped him off with the rest of his clothing. He was at first ashamed to have her see him and he admitted that he was worried because he was no Samson, but she kissed him and touched him and assured him that he had nothing in the world to worry about.

She lifted up the sheet and he crawled under it beside her. She kissed him and held him tight, moving gently against him so that her breasts rubbed into his chest. The hair on his chest tickled her and excited her.

Her heart was pounding and for a split second she wanted to hurry things, anxious to get the actual process started. But it was his first time and she wanted everything to be just right for him.

It began.

At first he was awkward and unsure of himself. Then the rhythm of love caught up with him and his heart beat in time with it and everything was just right, just right and as perfect as it could possibly be.

He was a wonderful lover. When it was finally over she held him against her for a long time, running tentative fingers over the small of his back and breathing in time with him. She took his head between her hands and kissed him chastely and warmly all over his face.

Now he was a man.

"Sheila—"

"What is it, honey?"

"I love you, Sheila."

"Don't say that!"

"Why not? It's the truth."

"Then don't let it be the truth. You mustn't love me, Harvey."

"But I do."

"Then stop it. I'm no good for you. I'm good for a roll in the hay but that's about all."

"You're very good. You're wonderful. You're the sweetest, most wonderful woman in the world."

She couldn't say anything.

"I want you with me," he said. "Not just what happened now. For everything—sitting with you, talking to you, even sitting here in the chair and watching you sleep. Everything about you—"

"Honey."

He looked at her.

"Honey, please don't fall in love with me. Can't you see what I am?"

"I know what you are," he said.

"And it doesn't bother you?"

"Of course it does," he said honestly. "But that's just a temporary thing. I'll be able to satisfy you. I'll bet I satisfied you before, didn't I?"

She wanted very much to lie.

But she couldn't.

When she had told him the truth he said: "But you acted as though—"

"I always act it out. But it never happens."

He forced a smile. "I'll take care of that," he said. "This time it will happen."

He took her—sure of himself now, sure of his manhood and sure of his love for her.

Sure that it would happen.

But it didn't.

She feigned orgasm, of course. She always did, both to make it better for the man and because the pretended release brought a certain measure of relief to her. And it must have been a good fake, because he was certain that he had brought her satisfaction.

When she told him the truth he buried his face between her warm breasts and cried like a baby.

CHAPTER 7

They were at Mitch's cottage. Madelaine had spent the greater part of three days in the careful process of avoiding Mitch, but to avoid her completely she would have had to stay in her room twenty-four hours of the day. Monday afternoon Mitch caught her walking down Commercial Street on the way back from lunch.

"Come on," she had said. "You've been dodging me like I had the pox or something. You better come and tell me about it anyway."

And so they had gone to the cottage. Now Mitch was sprawled on the bed while Madelaine sat prim and proper on the chair, her back straight as a rail and her knees pressed tightly together.

Madelaine explained everything very carefully. It would have been fairly easy to brush Mitch off without an explanation, but Madelaine felt compelled to tell the butch the whole truth. She explained everything—how she had been attracted to Sheila, how Sheila had ignored her, how she had hurried then to the Old Barn and taken Mitch out of a simple desire for sex.

Then she had avoided Mitch, feeling guilty over the way she had treated the other girl. She gave Mitch the full story while the butch listened in absolute silence, registering no emotions on her stolid face, making no sound and not nodding her head or moving her shoulders—in short, listening impassively to everything Madelaine had to say.

"Maddy," she said when Madelaine had finally finished, "you could have told me. For God's sake, you didn't have to run off without saying a word. Imagine how I felt when I woke up in the morning and you weren't there!"

"I'm sorry."

"Don't be sorry. It's just a shame—something must have been wrong with me that you didn't trust me enough to tell me then."

"There was nothing wrong with you. It was me, Mitch. I've always been selfish and—"

"Cut it out. Maddy, everybody's always selfish one hundred percent of the time. You can't do a thing without doing something selfish."

"What do you mean?"

"Just what I said. Look, give me an example of an unselfish act."

Madelaine thought for a minute. "All right," she said. "Suppose I gave a million dollars to charity."

"Why would you give it?"

"Out of the goodness of my heart."

"You'd give it because it made you feel better to give it. That's the only reason anybody ever gives anything to anybody. Maybe you'd give it to get rid of your own guilt feelings or to feel like a big shot or for any of a dozen reasons. But everything has to have a selfish reason."

"That's quite a generalization."

"Not really. It's more a semantic argument than anything

else—water doesn't flow uphill and people don't do things unless they're the things they want to do."

"I don't know if I can accept that."

Mitch shifted her position on the bed. "You don't have to," she said. "I think you will accept it if you think about it for awhile, but for the time being I just want you to stop worrying about being selfish."

Madelaine nodded.

Mitch's eyes narrowed. "Maddy," she said, "you've got one hell of a problem."

"I know."

"You're really in love with this doll?"

"I think so."

"You just met her that one time?"

"Yes."

"And fell in love with her on the spot?"

"That's right."

Mitch nodded. "That happens," she admitted. "Happens more with girls like us than with straight ones. We're so wrapped up in love on account of being different that we fall with a bang. It can be rough."

Mitch pulled a crumpled pack of Camels from the pocket of her leather jacket, offering one to Madelaine. Madelaine didn't smoke and shook her head to refuse the cigarette. Mitch put it between her own lips and snapped a match into flame. She drew on the cigarette and expelled a huge cloud of smoke. Then she looked at Madelaine.

"It can be even rougher," she said, "when the girl you fall for happens to be straight."

Madelaine didn't answer.

"You think this girl is straight?"

"She must be—I gave her a million openings. She was either straight or blind. Besides, I told you how she wound up the evening."

"Yeah."

"But I can't help thinking she's gay whether she knows it or not. I don't know, Mitch. I just can't help feeling that way. Call it intuition or something—that's the way she impressed me."

"Probably wishful thinking, honey. They all seem gay when you love them."

"Maybe."

"It's rough when they're straight."

"Did it ever happen to you that way?"

"Happens all the time. Hell, I'm a butch—it's natural for it to happen with me. The type of dolls I go for are the ultra-feminine type, so naturally a good portion of them are straight. Usually I just give up as soon as I find out."

"I see."

"But one time I didn't. It was pretty messy."

"What happened?"

Mitch hesitated. "You'll get sick of me if I tell you."

"Well . . . I raped the girl, Maddy."

Madelaine shuddered in spite of herself.

"It was pretty horrible. She hated me and she hated what I did to her. All the way through I was sure she'd like it if she gave herself the chance, but it turned out she was straight as an arrow all the way through. I felt like killing myself when it was over."

Madeline shuddered again. She could understand what Mitch meant.

"You going to try again with this Sheila?"

"I think so."

"Well, don't do what I did."

Madelaine chuckled. "I couldn't even if I wanted to. She's almost a foot taller than I am."

Mitch smiled. "Okay," she said. "I wish you all the luck in the world, and if you change your mind I'd love to see you again. I'm not in love with you, Maddy. I like you one hell of a lot and I like you in bed, but I'm not in love with you and for that reason we can still be friendly, even if you don't want to play lesbian games with me. I hope you make it with Sheila, but you better be careful. It's easy to get hurt."

"I know," she said. "I've been hurt before."

"Badly?"

"Pretty badly."

"Getting hurt is something you never get used to," Mitch said. "And no matter how badly you get hurt, it can always be a little bit worse the next time."

It was evening. Sheila sat alone at a tiny table in the rear of the Purple Oyster. From time to time she sipped Italian coffee from a demitasse cup. The coffee was thick and black and Harvey made it with an espresso machine. A sliver of lemon peel gave it an even more pungent taste and Sheila liked the flavor of it.

To all intents and purposes, she and Harvey were living together. While she still kept her clothing and belongings at her shack in the woods, she spent her nights in Harvey's bed with Harvey beside her.

She enjoyed sleeping with him. He had been a delightful lover from the first and continued practice only sharpened his enthusiasm and improved his technique. He remained gentle and considerate while he learned new variations and employed new methods to arouse her.

It was all very pleasant.

But it was a little frightening.

Being loved, Sheila discovered, was an unnerving experience. There were a number of very nice things about it. The love of another person was an extremely ego-building thing, to begin with. And she couldn't deny that the sense of emotional power over another human being was enjoyable at times.

But Harvey loved her with an all-consuming love, a love she was unable to return in full measure. And this was very irritating, to her as well as to him.

She looked up. He was behind the counter now preparing sandwiches, and she noticed how good he looked, how straight he stood and how handsome he was. If only she could love him as he loved her everything would be quite perfect. If only she could be his woman, his and his alone, then life would be quite delightful.

But that wasn't the case.

She was still Sheila Paine, still a nymphomaniac with an insatiable appetite and the moral development of an alley cat in heat. His love couldn't change that any more than her feeling for him could. So far she had remained true to him, but she knew very well that it was only a matter of time before another man came along and she took another step along the road to merry hell.

And he was such a good person! That just made everything worse. If he was selfish and possessive, if he made demands upon her, then she wouldn't feel so rotten about the way she knew she would ultimately disappoint him. But he *was* good and he *didn't* make demands upon her, and she felt like going off somewhere and drawing a thin, red line on her throat with a straight razor.

Sometimes he was so pathetic. That morning, for instance, he had almost worked himself into a heart attack in a valiant attempt to give her an orgasm. He seemed to think that sheer stamina would work the trick, and they wound up spending the whole morning in bed, going through every routine in the book with no result other than to leave him as exhausted as a man could be.

Then, after all that, he had asked her to marry him.

The funny part of it was that she had almost agreed. She came very close to going along with the idea, changing her mind just in time. The notion, on the surface, was a very attractive one. If she were married to Harvey he would take care of her. She would have one stable point in a basically unstable world, and maybe he would be able to straighten her out in time.

And he would be a tolerant husband, just as he was already a tolerant lover. He had even told her that she could make love with other men if she couldn't help herself, just so long as she didn't tell him about it. He was as understanding a person as she had ever met.

Then she realized how impossible such a marriage would be. It would wind up as an eternal source of agony and heartbreak to both of them. He would feel constantly miserable and inadequate because he wasn't enough of a man to satisfy her; she, on the other hand, would feel abysmally guilty every time she sought the solace of another lover.

No, it would never work out. It was better to keep it as it was—staying with him as long as he wanted her, living with him with no strings attached, and leaving him when he eventually tired of her. That was the only way they could both have each other and still remain reasonably sane.

She took another sip of her espresso, convinced that she had made the right decision. Harvey passed her with a tray full of food and drinks for a table of tourists sitting up front, and he winked at her as he walked by. She turned her head to watch him go.

The short brunette who walked into the Purple Oyster just then looked vaguely familiar to her, but she couldn't remember where she had seen her before.

Madelaine walked halfway into the café before she saw Sheila. She had walked into the Purple Oyster on the off-chance that the girl would be present, just as she had walked into half the bars and restaurants and shops in Provincetown that evening.

She had been looking, looking high and low and in and out and up and down. She had been looking for Sheila Paine, and now she had found her.

Now that the search was over she didn't know exactly what to do. Where did she go from here? She couldn't drop casual subtle hints; it was relatively simple to see that subtle hints would float miles over the head of the beautiful ash-blonde girl.

The Approach Obtuse was out of the question. The Approach Direct seemed to be called for in this situation, and Madelaine was worried that such an approach might do more harm than good. For a moment she stood very still in the middle of the café, not daring to look at Sheila, torn between twin desires to race over and embrace the girl and to turn tail and run like hell out of the place.

She didn't run over and fall on Sheila's neck. Neither did she leave. Instead she walked over very properly and seated herself across from the other girl. As she did so she realized that she was acting in much the same manner as that Bruce Ryerson had acted with her. She could only hope that she would prove less gauche and more successful than Ryerson.

"Do you remember me?" she asked quietly.

"I'm not sure."

"I'm Madelaine Carr," she said. "We met at a party at the Hookery."

"Now I remember."

"I've been wanting to see you ever since the party, Sheila."

"You have?"

Madelaine nodded, not trusting herself to speak for the moment. God, everything was getting messed up! She had to word all this in the proper manner, but the Lord only knew what the proper manner was. With another lesbian she could just come out and speak her piece, but now she felt as though her tongue was tied behind her back. Mitch had been right—the whole thing was utterly impossible.

But just sitting across from Sheila, just looking at that beautiful face and imagining her own lips pressing against those soft red lips . . .

"Where are you from, Sheila?"

"Georgia, originally."

"Really? You talk like New England."

"My parents lived in Lowell before I was born. We moved back when I was fourteen, so any southern accent I had is long gone by now."

"Then you live in Lowell now?"

"No—Boston."

"Really? That's a coincidence—I'm from Boston myself. Whereabouts do you live?"

Sheila told her, wondering what all this was about. It didn't make a hell of a lot of sense to her, but she didn't know what to do other than to carry on a conversation with the girl.

"Why, I live just a few blocks from you, Sheila. Isn't it strange that we had to come all the way out to the end of the Cape before we ran into each other!"

Sheila agreed that it was strange.

"Just imagine," Madelaine said, not quite sure what it was that she wanted the blonde girl to imagine. She was stalling for time, anxious to get the necessary words spoken but mortally afraid of the reaction she couldn't help expecting. She looked down at her hands and noticed that her fingers were trembling visibly.

She put her hands in her lap.

"What—"

"Sheila," she broke in, "I have to talk to you."

"Go ahead."

"Could we go someplace a little more private?"

"What's the matter with right here?"

"It's awfully . . . public for what I have to say. Couldn't we go somewhere else?"

"Well, the man I'm with is working here and . . ."

"It will only take a minute or so. We could just step outside."

"Well," Sheila said. "All right—but just for a few minutes."

Madelaine stood up; then Sheila did the same. The short girl walked directly to the door while Sheila went to the counter to tell Harvey she would be outside for a few minutes. Then she joined Madelaine on the sidewalk.

"Look," she said, "if you think I have the slightest idea what this is all about you're wrong. I wish you'd set me straight."

Madelaine hesitated. She would have to lay it on the line; that was all there was to it. But she was so scared, so damnably scared.

"All right," she said. "All right."

Sheila waited.

"I'm . . . I'm—"

She couldn't say it.

"Yes?"

In one breath she said: "I'm a lesbian."

A long period of frightful silence.

"Well," Sheila said. "Congratulations."

Madelaine couldn't move, couldn't breathe, couldn't say a word. At least it was out, at least there would be no more word games from here on in. But the expression on Sheila's face could hardly be called encouraging.

"You're a lesbian?"

She nodded.

"So what?"

Why did Sheila have to make it so hard for her? Why was everything turning out so badly? Things should have moved smoothly—communication, understanding, sympathy, love, one following the other in an orderly chain that led to a bedroom and two hungry bodies giving and taking and making the sweetest music in the world.

But that wasn't what was happening.

"I want—"

Sheila stared at her impatiently.

"I want to sleep with you."

There.

Now it was out.

Sheila's eyes narrowed and furrows appeared on her forehead. "You do?"

"Yes."

"What makes you think I want to sleep with you?"

"I—"

"What happened at the party—is that what it is? You think just because I took on every man in the state of Massachusetts that I'm a dirty little pervert who lets anybody come along and get her on a bed? Is that what you think?"

"No! No, I—"

"I've done a lot of things, damn it. A lot of things I shouldn't have done. But I'm not a stinking queer, do you understand? *I'm not a queer!*"

A couple turned to stare at them.

"Please," Madelaine was saying. "Please—"

"Why don't you leave me alone?"

Madelaine's knees were shaking and she wished she could die right then and there, die and disappear into the pavement and not have to live through this. It was so horrible, so indescribably horrible, and it was going as wrong as anything could possibly go.

"Please—"

"*Why?*"

Softly: "Because I love you."

Sheila's hands knotted into fists and her fingernails bit into her palms. "You love me," she said. "Everybody loves me. Everybody in the whole goddamned world loves me."

"But I do—"

"Shut up." Her eyes blazed. "Listen to me," she said. "Listen to me and don't miss a word of this. You'd better get it straight right away from start to finish because I don't want to have to repeat it."

She paused for a breath.

"I'm not a dirty queer," she said. "I didn't take you for one, either, because you sure as hell look feminine enough. I suppose I should have known, the way you came up to me at that party and all, but I was too drunk to notice a damned thing.

"But I'm telling you now, I'm not interested in anything that you're interested in. I don't want to see you and I don't want to talk to you and I sure as hell don't want to go to bed with you. I don't want to have anything to do with you—do you understand that? Not a thing!"

Tears welled up behind Madelaine's eyes.

"Now get away from me! Get away and stay away or so help me I'll kill you. Do you understand? I'm not a queer!"

Madelaine turned away. She tried to walk but her feet didn't seem to respond. She took one step, then another, and finally she was walking normally. For a block and a half her body shook with terror and she could barely breathe. Then she had control of herself and walked the rest of the way home without any trouble.

In her own room with the door closed and bolted she cried for forty-five minutes without a break.

CHAPTER 8

Sheila was still shaking in a weird combination of horror and cold fury. Espresso spilled from the cup when she raised it to her lips and her face was pale and drawn. But her eyes blazed like fiery coals burning themselves up in a heap of fresh snow.

"God," she said. "I was never so furious—"

"Take it easy, honey."

"How can I take it easy? When you stop to think what that woman wanted me to do—"

Harvey reached across the table and patted her hand. His eyes assured her that he understood completely.

"I shouldn't call her a woman," Sheila said. "She's not a woman. She's some kind of unnatural monster. She's a filthy queer, that's what she is. Just thinking about what she wanted is enough to make me sick to my stomach. The colossal nerve of that . . . that dike!"

"It's okay, Sheila."

"Dammit, it's not okay! People like her ought to be locked up, and whoever locks them up ought to throw the key into the ocean. Then they should forget which ocean they threw it into just to make sure. My God, you wouldn't have thought it to look at her. She's such a pretty little thing on the surface."

"Not as pretty as you are."

She smiled at him and her own hand covered his and squeezed it. "You're sweet," she said.

Then her face went serious again and the smile evaporated. "Honey," she said, "I'm not kidding about that . . . that girl. I'm serious. There ought to be some way to get her out of this town."

"Don't be silly, Sheila."

"Silly?"

"Yes, silly."

"Is it silly to—"

"Provincetown has a large percentage of homosexuals, both male and female," he explained. "Almost any town like this one does. They keep to themselves most of the time and they rarely bother anyone."

"Well, she bothered me."

"Evidently she was strongly attracted to you—I can't blame her. But I don't think she'll bother you any more."

"She better not."

"Don't worry about it," he said. "I'll close up in a little while and we'll go on home. Then you can forget all about lesbians."

"You think so?"

"Yes.

She smiled. "What makes you so sure?"

He said: "I'll give you something else to think about."

But when he did finally close the Purple Oyster for the night they did not return to his cottage. The night was warm, with a moon that was nearly full and a sky full of stars. It was a good night for love but it was a bad night to be cooped up inside. It was definitely a night to be outdoors.

So they spent it outdoors.

They took her car and drove to the beach, the same beach that she had met Greg at not too long ago. Naturally the beach was deserted, and with the moon's reflection floating on the calm water it was strikingly beautiful.

She had a blanket in the trunk and they spread it out on the sand. Silently they sat down side by side on the blanket and his arms went around her at once, holding her, clutching her to him. Their lips met and pressed together, seeking each other, giving and taking and exchanging sweetness and love under the gleaming moon. Her mind whirled. She thought suddenly and inevitably of Madeline and she kissed Harvey with sudden ferocity, furious all at once at the nerve of the lesbian. How could any woman dare to make a pass at her?

With only the moon and the stars as an audience they took off their clothes. The water was freezing cold against bare flesh and they could only stay out in it for a little while. Sheila swam around like a champion, but by the time she came out onto the beach she was freezing.

She knew a good way to get warm again.

Wet naked bodies together. Bodies slippery from the sea, embracing, grinding, moving, pitching mutual passion higher and higher.

They slept in each other's arms, slept nude on the beach with the stars over them and the blanket under them, slept deeply and dreamed of love.

•   •   •

The sun woke them a few minutes before six. Sheila woke and stretched, feeling life returning to her love-tired muscles, tasting salty air in her lungs and relishing the warmth of early morning sun on naked flesh.

"Hey," she said. She rolled over and touched Harvey, touched his lean young body and smiled as his eyes opened.

"You just wake up?"

"Uh-huh."

"I woke up a while back but you were still sleeping so I left you alone. Guess I dozed off again."

"Guess so."

"Last night was nice," he said. "Last night was pretty great, as a matter of fact."

"Glad you enjoyed yourself."

"It was the end of the world," he said. "Did anybody ever tell you that you were the most beautiful woman in the entire world."

"Yes," she said. "Someone did."

"Who was he?"

"A guy named Harvey Chase."

"Perceptive son of a bitch."

"That's not all he is."

"It isn't?"

"Nope," she said.

"What else is he?"

"Sexy."

"Yeah?"

"Yeah."

"Oh," he said. "You know, inspire me. I think I'll write a poem."

"Go ahead."

> He said: *"I know that I shall never feel a*
> *Breast that's shaped like that of Sheila."*

She took his hand and placed it on her breast, feeling her nipple harden against his palm. "That's a nice poem," she said.

"It's a nice breast. But there's more to the poem."

"Oh—go ahead."

> He said: *"I'd give my right arm just to steal a*
> *Kiss from that fair maiden, Sheila."*

"Maiden?" she said, arching an eyebrow.

"What the hell—poetic license."

She kissed him.

"I wish you'd stop interrupting me," he said. "There's more to the poem."

"Let's hear it."

> He said: *"I'd risk a bite from many a Gila*
> *Monster just to fondle Sheila."*

She bit him.

"Ouch!"

"Sorry. Any more to the poem?"

"I'm afraid that's all so far."

"Oh," she said. "I like your poem."

"Then you ought to give me a reward."

"What kind of a reward did you have in mind?"

"Oh, I don't know."

She grinned. "Can't you think of anything you'd like?"

"Well—"

She wrapped her arms around his neck and pulled him down

to her, pressing his lips against hers. Then she wriggled around on the blanket so that his mouth was pressed to her breast. His tongue ran over her nipple and she squirmed around some more, her hands roaming over his back.

"Hey," he said. "I just got a great idea."

"What is it?"

"Let's make love."

"That's a pretty original idea. You always manage to come up with something nice and new. Something we have never done before."

"As a matter of fact," he said, "I do happen to have a new idea."

"You do?"

"I do," he said, tugging playfully on her nipple with his teeth.

"Ouch!"

"That hurt?"

"Damn right it hurt."

"Good," he said. "I wanted it to hurt. Don't you want to hear my new idea?"

"I'd love to hear it if you'd stop biting my breasts."

He bit her again.

"Oww!"

"Here's the idea," he said. "Let's make love in the water."

"Huh?"

He repeated it.

"In the water?"

"Sure—why not?"

"I don't think it's possible."

"Ever try it?"

"No," she admitted. "But—"

"Don't you think it's worth a try?"

"I suppose so."

"Then let's give it a try."

"Okay," she said. "That old college try."

They stood up and walked to the water.

"How far out should we go?"

"Not too far," he said. "We might get carried away and drown ourselves."

"Right here okay?"

"This is fine."

They were standing in a foot and a half of water. She decided as she sat down in the water that what they were about to do was no doubt quite impossible, but the way her heart was beating she didn't want to waste time worrying about it.

Making love in the water turned out to be quite possible.

And quite enjoyable.

They did it a second time just for the sheer hell of it.

It was good that making love in the water was enjoyable.

The rest of the day was anything *but* enjoyable.

The rest of the day was hell.

They dried off about eight o'clock and got dressed before anybody else arrived on the beach. The blanket was shaken out and tossed into the trunk and the two of them hopped into the front seat of the car and drove into town. It wasn't time yet to open the Purple Oyster, so they drove to Harvey's cottage to change clothes.

That's when it started.

She was sitting on the bed; he was stepping into a pair of khaki pants. One moment everything was fine and the next moment everything was not fine at all.

She could sense what he was about to say almost before he said it. His eyes got a funny look in them and she knew all at once what was coming.

Marriage.

"Sheila," he said evenly, "I think it's time we talked about getting married."

"Oh," she said.

"Don't you think so?"

"No, Harvey. I don't."

He sat down in the chair.

"Honey," he said, "I'm in love with you. I don't have to tell you that. You're the first woman I've loved and I've loved you since I first met you, since that first time we made love right here on the bed you're sitting on now. I haven't stopped loving you and I know I never will."

"Harvey—"

"Let me finish, Sheila. I need you—I need you terribly and I don't think I could get along if I didn't have you. You don't know how lonely I was before, Sheila. Even I didn't realize how miserable I was, and I have to have you or else I'll—"

"But you do have me," she cut in.

"You know what I mean."

She was silent.

"I need you on a permanent basis," he said. "Not this day-to-day sort of affair—it's good, it's wonderful, I'm happier than I've ever been in my life, but it just isn't enough. I want you for my wife. I want to plant children inside you and watch them grow up. I want—"

She got a mental picture of herself as Harvey's wife, pregnant with his children. She thought of herself as a mother and a wife.

The picture looked ridiculous, impossible to attain.

"I want you forever," he was saying. "That's the way it has to be."

"It can't be that way."

"Why not?"

She didn't know how to answer. How could she make him see how impossible it all was? How could she make him realize that she was a girl to have fun with but not a girl to marry? How could she get him to drop the subject once and for all without hurting him?

She didn't know how.

So she waited for him to go on.

He began pacing back and forth on the cottage floor, taking four steps in one direction and four steps back. He paced in cold silence, not looking at her, not speaking to her. Then he stopped and threw himself down into the chair, his eyes accusing her, his face drawn and tired looking.

"You've got to marry me," he said. "That's all there is to it."

"I can't."

"Don't say you can't, Sheila. You can if you want to. It's very simple—we get a ring and a license and a justice of the peace and the next thing you know we're married. Don't say you can't because you can. Say you don't want to."

"All right—I don't want to."

"Why not?"

"Because it's impossible."

"What's impossible about it?"

"It just is—that's all."

"That's what you said about loving in shallow water. Sometimes if you give something a try you find out that it works out."

"Harvey—"

"What?"

"Harvey, I just don't want to get married. Not to you or to anybody else in the world. Not for a good long time and probably not forever. Can't you understand that?"

"*Why?*"

"You don't have to shout at me."

"I'm sorry. I didn't mean to."

He stood up again and began pacing the floor—back and forth, back and forth. Then he stopped and stared at her.

"I love you," he said.

She didn't say anything.

"And you love me," he said. "Don't you?"

She didn't answer.

"Don't you?"

She wanted to tell him she did. She wanted very much to tell him, to tell him right away and then to prove it to him right there on the bed she was sitting on.

That's what she wanted to do.

But she couldn't do it.

"No," she said. "I don't love you, Harvey. I wish to hell I did but I don't."

"Yes you do."

She didn't answer.

"You must," he said. "You're in love with me without realizing it. You must be."

"I—"

"Look," he said, "sex is what's bothering you, isn't it? That's the main thing—right?"

"I suppose so."

"Listen," he told her, "I think you've got this built up in your mind past the point where it makes any sense. You make a big thing about needing so many men. Now we've been together for a little while now, haven't we?"

She nodded, sensing what was coming and hoping that it wouldn't.

"You haven't . . . had sexual relations with anybody else in the time we've been together, have you?"

"No," she said.

"And you haven't wanted to, either."

It was a statement, not a question. As such it didn't seem to call for an answer.

So she didn't say anything.

Then: "Well, *have* you?"

There was a long pause. Then she heard him repeat the question. Her heart was racing and her hands were trembling and she wished desperately that she could lie. If only she didn't have this overpowering compulsion to be truthful with him things would be simpler all across the board. Maybe she couldn't help telling the truth because she was fond of him—maybe that was it.

What she said was: "Yes, I have."

"You have?"

"Constantly," she said, closing her eyes so she wouldn't have to look at the expression on his face. "Every other man I look at. I can't help wondering what it would be like and wanting to . . . to sleep with him and—"

"Stop it!"

She opened her eyes.

"Sheila, I can't take it any more. You're kidding, aren't you?"

"No," she said softly. "I'm not kidding."

"Then what in the name of God is the matter with you? You sound as though you're just a rotten little slut. Is that all you are?"

His words hurt but she didn't flinch.

"Yes," she said. "That's what I'm trying to tell you. I'm just a rotten little slut."

She was very calm now. She knew that what they had was beginning to explode in her face but somehow she was ready for the explosion. She breathed easily and her heart was beating at what seemed to be a normal rate. She could look at him without feeling anything but a quiet sorrow, could listen to what he had to say without trembling or shaking or worrying or crying.

What he had to say did not make pleasant listening. For awhile he shouted at her and called her names; then he would apologize and fall on his knees and place his head in her lap, begging forgiveness and intensifying his pleas that she marry him.

She listened to all of it. From beginning to end, from start to finish, the whole two hours worth of alternating curses and praises.

In between she assured him over and over again that he didn't love her, or that if he did it was a love he would get over with in a short enough span of time. She had been the first woman for him—naturally he felt strongly about her. But he was confusing sex with love, and as soon as he found somebody else he would get over her and forget about her.

He didn't believe her, of course, and she knew he wouldn't believe her, and the whole scene was impossible all along. But it was something she had to tell him.

It was even worse toward the end. By that time he too must have realized that it was all over between them, and in a last effort to hold their relationship together he became very cruel to her. He called her every name he could think of from *nymphomaniac* to *whore of Babylon*, shouted at her until he was blue in the face.

Then he hit her.

It was probably more to prove his manhood than anything else, to prove his manhood and let off some of the steam that had been building up within him. With one hand he lifted her to her feet. Then he slapped her across the face with his other hand— hard, ringing slaps that made her head spin dizzily.

He released her and drove his balled-up fist into her stomach, sending the wind gushing from her lungs and hurting her terribly. She gasped in pain and he struck her again harder than before.

Then, strangely, they made love. It was a weird and terrible love, composed of equal parts of love and hate, a frightening, fast and furious experiment in mutual misery that left him tired and spent, lying upon her but miles away from her. They said nothing, but both of them knew now that it had been the last time, that they would never see each other again.

Something, she wasn't sure just what, had existed between them. Something that was good.

Something that was over, over and done with.

He said nothing to her while she dressed or while she was

picking up what clothing she had left at his place. Then she straightened up and headed for the door.

He didn't try to stop her.

She got in her car, heading for her own cabin. The top was down on the convertible and the wind whistled through her long blonde hair.

She felt empty, wasted, dead.

CHAPTER 9

She couldn't sleep.

It was strange, she thought. It should be easy enough for her to lie down on her concave bed and stare at the rafters until sleep came. She and Harvey had only had a few hours sleep on the beach the night before, and here it was eight o'clock in the evening and she still wasn't asleep, not that eight o'clock was so late but she was tired and there was nothing to do but sleep. So why, why in the world couldn't she fall asleep?

Sleep would be good. *The innocent sleep, sleep that knits up the raveled sleeve of care, the death of each day's life, sore labor's bath, balm of hurt minds, great nature's second course, chief nourisher in life's feast*—Shakespeare was right. Sleep was the obvious recourse when you felt horrible and empty and vile and there was absolutely nothing that you wanted to do.

But she couldn't sleep.

At eight-thirty she gave up. She dragged herself out of bed and put on her clothes, dressing hurriedly in a grey skirt and a red blouse. The blouse was tight around her breasts and a bit too small for her, while the skirt hugged her hips a bit too snugly. Besides the color combination wasn't the best in the world. But she didn't much care—she would only be gone for a minute or two and probably wouldn't run into anybody anyway, and even if she did it didn't make one hell of a lot of difference. There was nobody in the whole town that she gave much of a damn about. If she looked like hell, let them all turn and look the other way. Sheila Paine couldn't have cared less.

She left the cottage and locked the door after her. Her car was parked in its usual spot and she opened the door and slid behind the wheel. For once she didn't even bother putting the top down. She rarely drove with it up, unless the rain made topless driving too uncomfortable. Normally the wind in her hair felt good.

This time she didn't care.

She drove, top up and windows shut, into the center of town. Without much trouble she found the place she was looking for and found a parking place right in front of the store. She parked expertly, got out, locked the door again, and went into the store.

An old man, weather-beaten and gray, sat behind the counter on a rickety wooden stool. His face was creased and his clothing rumpled, and his general appearance suggested that somebody had crumpled him up in an untidy little ball and left him for several months at the bottom of a drawer full of soiled clothing. A skimpy white moustache perched upon his upper lip and the ends drooped sadly.

"Yep?" he said, expectantly.

"I'd like a bottle of liquor."

"Yep—that's what I'm here to sell you."

She waited, wondering what he was waiting for. Why didn't he just get up and sell her the liquor instead of sitting there with a stupid expression on his face?

"Miss—"

She frowned at him.

"Mind telling me what kind of liquor you'd be wanting?"

She flushed, embarrassed. "Bourbon," she said.

"Any special brand?"

"Anything—I don't care."

"This Jack Daniels is the best around, Miss. Can't buy a better bourbon no matter how hard you look. Best stuff you'll find anywhere."

"All right," she said. "That will be fine."

"Want a fifth or a pint?"

"You better make it a fifth."

"Only trouble with the Jack Daniels," he said, "is it's so danged expensive. Cost you around seven bucks for the fifth. You might not want to spend that much."

She didn't say anything.

"Now this J.W. Dant—this is bonded, too. Good bourbon and it's lots cheaper. If you'd rather have the Dant—"

"All right," she said. "I'll take the Dant."

"Unless," the man drawled, "unless you'd be wanting something a little milder. Now the Dant's a hundred proof, you know, and a lot of ladies like something that goes down a little easier. We got this Jim Beam in—it's also a very good buy, good bourbon for the money only it ain't the regular hundred proof. Maybe you'd—"

Hopelessly she said: "Please, could you just give me a fifth of bourbon? I don't honestly care what kind it is or what proof or anything. If you could just give it to me in a hurry I'd be eternally grateful."

"I'm sorry," he said. "I was just trying to help you out, give you a helping hand so to speak. No need to get so rickety about it."

"I—"

"All I'm saying is I think there's three brands you should choose from—the Daniels if you want the best, or the Dant, or the Beam if you like a lighter whiskey. I didn't mean to rile you or anything—"

He broke off and sat there, the three fifths of whiskey in front of him with a hurt expression on his face.

"I'll take the Jack Daniels," she said, feeling angry with herself and sorry for him.

He put the bottle in a bag while she placed a ten dollar bill on the counter and waited for change. He gave her the bottle and the change. She put the change in her purse and held the bottle desperately between her hands.

"That all, Miss?"

"I think so."

"Hope you enjoy it."

"Thank you." She turned and fled from the store, getting her key into the lock without wasting any time and gunning the car back toward the cabin.

Everything seemed to be working out so horribly. She was well rid of Harvey, she knew, and the depression she felt at having lost him was less sorrow over his loss than it was a deep and abiding feeling of self-pity. She was indulging in the pleasant pastime of feeling sorry for herself, only in this case it wasn't especially pleasant. It was, to be truthful, a miserable way to pass the time.

What in the world was a nymphomaniac supposed to do? It was easy to see that a normal life was outside the pale for her.

She just couldn't live that way—husband, kids, white house with green shutters—things didn't happen that way, not if your name was Sheila Paine.

If your name was Sheila Paine you flitted from man to man and never stayed anywhere long enough to begin to fall in love. The longer you forced yourself to stay with a man, the more painful it was all across the board when you finally ran out on him. That's what had happened with Harvey—if she had been smart, she decided, she would have laid him and left him right at the beginning. Agreeing to live with him, however enjoyable it was at the onset, was one hell of a mistake for her.

She parked the car again, got out of it and locked it. Then, her right hand clenched in a death grip around the paper-covered neck of the bourbon bottle, she made her way back to her cabin along the primeval path. She hesitated at the door before unlocking it, wishing that there was some other place to go than the cabin and some other way to pass the night than in the sweet-and-sour oblivion of the bourbon bottle.

Of course she could go out and find a man. That wouldn't be hard; not for her. She had the skill and the practice. All she had to do was wiggle her pretty tail and give a shake of her ash-blonde hair and there would be a man around her, a man who was more than willing to give her something to forget with.

No.

No, not tonight, she thought fiercely. Not a man, not tonight, not so soon after he's gone. Her loins warmed at the thought of a man but, simultaneously, something within her recoiled at the same thought.

She turned the key in the lock, went into the cabin and turned to bolt the door. Then she changed her mind—leaving the door open would be the element of chance in the evening's entertainment. If nobody came to the door, then her night would be passed in peaceful celibacy. And if someone should come, then he could have her—be he ten-year-old boy, seventy-year-old roué, or escaped sex maniac.

She kicked off her shoes and sat down on the bed. There was, she knew, a clean or almost-clean glass in the kitchen. But she didn't feel like walking even that far.

She took the bottle from the bag and dropped the empty paper bag to the floor. With steady fingers she peeled the seal from the cap and opened the bottle, raising it at once to her lips.

The Jack Daniels was all the old codger has said it was—the best bourbon she had ever tasted. It went right down her throat and tasted like bourbon mixed with honey, smooth and mild and full and rich. Normally she gagged when she took a big drink of straight liquor but this stuff was like drinking water—except for the taste, which wasn't like water at all.

She took another drink. The second drink tasted even better than the first, which was going some.

The third drink tasted better than the second.

She sat on the edge of the bed, the bottle still in her hand, a quiet smile on her lips. She was waiting for the liquor to take effect and wondering what in the world she would do when the bottle was empty.

Madelaine Carr knew too many things.

That, Madelaine decided, was the trouble. Just this afternoon she had found out where Sheila Paine lived, and she had found that out almost by accident. Early that morning she had gone over to the wharf to rent a bicycle, thinking that some exercise might take her mind off herself. Then around and around on the bicycle, her legs bare below the striped Bermuda shorts, her cotton blouse billowing in the breeze as her legs pumped hard and the bike covered the ground rapidly.

It was good exercise. She cycled all over town, then headed out Route Six a ways and pedaled hard. Finally about noon she turned around and headed back.

She saw Sheila's ear parked in front of Harvey's cottage and thought at first that Sheila lived there. Then, standing by the side of her bike and feeling sick at the memory of the night before, she saw Sheila dash out of the house and hop into the car.

Sheila drove slowly, slowly enough so that Madelaine could keep the green convertible in sight without too much trouble. She was riding an English racer, a boy's bike because they happened to be out of girl's bikes at the time she rented it, and she remembered thinking that it was vaguely appropriate that she was riding a boy's bike as she followed Sheila. After all, the only difference between the two was that you couldn't ride a boy's bike with a skirt on. When you were wearing Bermudas it didn't make a hell of a great difference which kind of bike you were riding.

She followed Sheila to the place where the blonde girl parked her car. Then she watched her go up the path to the ramshackle cabin.

Now it was well after nine, with the sky dark and the moon pale in the sky. Now she was back in her own room and sitting in her own chair, and now if she had a brain in her head she would leave her room with her suitcase clutched tightly in her hot little hand and get the next bus out of there.

There was a bus to Hyannis in an hour or so. From there she could get a bus to Boston and that would be the end of the Provincetown expedition in short order. Back to the heat of midsummer Boston—it would be hot as Hades, but wasn't that better than what she was going through in P-town?

Because, while P-town might be several degrees cooler than Hades, it was much closer to Hell in other respects.

Queer.

That was what Sheila had called her. And, strangely enough, it left her firmly convinced that Sheila Paine wasn't anywhere near as straight as she seemed to think she was. Whether Sheila Paine knew it or not, she was a lesbian.

She had to be, Madelaine felt. She knew both from her reading and from her own experience that severe fear and hatred of homosexuality was the surest sign of latent homosexuality. If a girl like Sheila hated "queers" as much as she did, it was almost definitely because, consciously or subconsciously, she was afraid of the streak of lesbianism in her own self. Only fear could make a girl that vicious, that cruel, that vindictive.

But this marvelous realization didn't do too much for Madelaine's peace of mind. She herself was easily convinced of Sheila's potential in the gay world—that was natural, since she was dying to be convinced.

Convincing Sheila was another matter entirely.

She wanted to leave Provincetown. She wanted to get out at once, or at the very least to catch the boat to Boston in the morning. That would be a lot more pleasant than the bus trip. But could she trust herself if she didn't get out right away?

For a moment she decided that she couldn't, that the only thing to do was to get out at the first opportunity. She even went so far as to get her small suitcase from the closet and to prop it open on the bed. She had an armful of clothing in her hand before she changed her mind and returned the clothes to the bureau drawer, closing the suitcase and replacing it in the closet.

She had two alternatives. She could go home or she could try once again to get Sheila to accept the love she was so willing to give her. The third alternative, which consisted of staying in Provincetown while staying away from Sheila, was sure to prove impossible. It was only a postponement of the choice—she wouldn't be able to remain in the same town with the girl for long before she made another approach to her.

Like a sleepwalker she left her room and went down the staircase to the first floor. Like a sleepwalker she left her rooming house and walked toward Sheila's cabin. When she had reached the spot where Sheila's car was parked she stood still in her tracks for several minutes, wishing that she could stop herself and turn around and run.

She couldn't.

Her feet were steady and her hands moved easily at her sides as she followed the path to the blonde girl's cabin. To all appearances she was perfectly cool and perfectly calm, just one pretty girl on her way to visit another pretty girl. Inwardly she was a mess. She didn't know what she could say or what she could do, and she fully expected another harsh rebuff like the one she had received the other night.

She kept walking.

Madelaine stood for several seconds at the closed door. She listened carefully, but there were no sounds coming from the little cabin. For a second or two she wanted very much to turn and leave, but turning and leaving were all in all quite impossible.

When she knocked, timidly at first, on the door, no answer came from within. She knocked again, louder than the first time, and again her knock went unanswered.

A third knock.

No answer.

Could Sheila be out? The car was there—she ought to be at home, unless somebody had come for her and had picked her up.

On the off-chance that she was at home Madelaine gave a little push at the closed door.

The door swung open.

At first she didn't see Sheila. Her eyes scanned the small room, quickly without lighting on the familiar form of the big and beautiful blonde.

Then she saw her.

Sheila was lying on the floor at the side of the bed. An empty liquor bottle lay a few inches from the outstretched fingers of her right hand. She was slumped down, her head resting awkwardly against the side of the bed, her legs stretched out awkwardly. Her feet were bare.

For a horrible instant Madelaine thought that the girl was dead. She rushed over to her, her fingers groping for Sheila's wrist.

There was a pulse. Sheila was alive; very much alive, although the liquor had knocked her thoroughly unconscious. And it was no wonder—by the looks of things the girl had knocked off a cool fifth of bonded bourbon. That was enough to put just about anybody under the table.

Madelaine didn't know what to do. The smart thing, she thought, would be to leave. But she couldn't leave the girl she loved lying on the floor fully dressed. Sheila might catch cold or worse. She had to put her to bed.

It wasn't easy getting her on top of the bed. Sheila was heavy to begin with and Madelaine was small and not very strong. Drunk as she was, Sheila was inert and seemed to weigh twice as much as she really did, just as a corpse always seems heavier than a live person. But finally Madelaine managed to get her on top of the sheet. She started to pull the blanket up to cover the blonde girl, then stopped suddenly.

No, she couldn't let her sleep in her clothes like that. She would get all sweaty, especially sweating out all that liquor. That wouldn't be good.

Her hands trembled as she undressed Sheila. Her fingers shook as she first unbuttoned the tight red blouse, then turned the girl over onto her stomach and slipped it over her shoulders. Sheila had dressed quickly; she wasn't wearing a bra, and the expanse of golden flesh made Madelaine's head whirl crazily.

Then the skirt. Once more Madelaine rolled Sheila over, this time onto her back. Her hands were unsure and excited, but she managed to master the hook-and-eye attachment and the zipper.

She took off the skirt.

Sheila had dressed in a very great hurry; there was nothing under the skirt, nothing but Sheila. The girl was nude and magnificent from her ash-blonde hair down past her thrusting breasts and flat stomach, past more ash-blonde hair to thighs and calves and feet. Nude and magnificent, nude and beautiful, nude and desirable.

Nude and defenseless.

No, no, no, no, no. Madelaine wanted to leave, wanted to pull the covers up and run from the room.

She wanted to—but she couldn't.

Her fingers shaking, she reached out one hand and let it rest on Sheila's breasts. The girl didn't awaken and her breast was firm and soft and absolutely wonderful to touch, the sweetest, warmest, most perfect breast that Madelaine had ever held in her hand. Aimlessly she traced small circles with her index finger on the breast, circling the nipple and exciting herself past the point of no return.

She straightened up, her back so stiff that the muscles ached in it. She hated herself now, hated herself for what she was and for what she was about to do. But she knew also that there was no way in the world for her to stop herself.

She began to undress. She removed all of her clothing quickly and methodically until her small white body was as nude as the large golden body on the bed.

She lay down on the bed. The two beautiful feminine bodies lay inches apart. They were not touching, not yet, but the smaller girl could feel the warmth of Sheila's body heat on her own bare skin.

For several minutes Madelaine didn't move at all. It was enough for the moment just to be with Sheila, to lie close to her, to listen to her shallow breathing and to watch and delight in the rise and fall of the girl's breasts.

Then she grew warm with desire and it was no longer enough to look. Her body burned with the need for the sweet fulfillment and release that Sheila and only Sheila could give her.

She rolled over so that her body was pressed tight to Sheila's. The thought that the girl might wake up tore her apart but she could hold herself back no longer. Her hungry mouth was everywhere—planting hot searing kisses on Sheila's lips and throat, travelling downward, downward. Then she took Sheila in her arms so that her own small firm breasts pressed against the large firm breasts of the sleeping girl, took her in her arms and gripped Sheila's body tight against her own. She placed Sheila's limp right hand against her burning cheek and put her own hands where she had longed so desperately to place them.

Her breathing doubled and trebled and she was wrapped up in the ecstasy of love, wrapped up in it and tossed headlong into a maelstrom of dizzying sensations.

Sheila moaned—a tiny little noise that came from deep within her throat, a moan that might have been the product of some remote and secret dream. Madelaine was afraid the girl would wake up before she had finished, but she could no more stop herself than she could cause her own heart to slow down.

Her body was screaming with a tortured hunger for relief. She prayed that Sheila would sleep on, just for a minute more, just for one more minute.

Then Sheila woke up. Her eyes said that she knew everything that was happening and the shock in them was too much for Madelaine to bear.

A second later the alcohol hit her and she was unconscious once again.

And seconds after that Madelaine was done, and then she was slipping from the bed to the floor, slipping away from Sheila and away from herself, her eyes overflowing with tears of both joy and sorrow.

CHAPTER 10

Walking.

A long walk, with the moon over her and the ground under her, with a breeze tossing her hair and the road stretching out in front of her like a supine snake waiting for the right moment to strike.

Walking.

She was bad—bad and evil inside, rotten like an apple half-eaten by worms, rotten and foul-smelling and no good to anybody. She hated herself, hated herself so much that she wanted to rip off her arms and hit herself over the head with them until she managed to dash out what brains she possessed.

Madelaine walked along, hating herself, hating the world, empty inside as a vacant room, empty and void of all but the ever-present self hatred. She walked past the edge of town, out onto the ribbon of highway by the sea, out past the last lonely cottage into comparative wilderness.

She was no better than Mitch, she decided. She was worse than Mitch, worse than anything that had ever lived. Mitch had raped a girl; she had raped a girl while the girl slept. She had made love to Sheila Paine while liquor had dulled the girl's brain past the point of recognition.

What kind of a woman could take advantage of a sleeping girl? What kind of beast could make love to a partner who was unaware of what was happening, who would never have permitted it if she had known about it?

What kind of a woman?

A bad and evil woman, she answered herself. A bad, rotten, foul woman who let her loins make the decisions her mind should have been making, a snake-in-a-woman's body. A foul, heartless and soulless woman.

A queer.

She hated everything about herself, hated her slender and pretty body, hated her breasts and her thighs, hated her sex. She hated herself, and there was only one thing to do with something that was hateful and foul.

Destroy it.

Taking the boat to Boston wouldn't be enough. Taking the bus to Hyannis wouldn't do the trick. She would still be Madelaine Carr, still the sexual freak who queered up everybody's life including her own. And she would still love Sheila Paine, love her with a hopeless and horrible love that could bring nothing but agony to whoever it touched upon.

There was only one way, one method that would end her misery forever.

Suicide.

She had thought of suicide before, of course, and she doubted that there was a homosexual in the world, male or female, who hadn't at one time or other considered taking his or her own life. She had conceived of the notion that first night years ago when Lita Barnstable had made her aware of the sort of woman she was, and the notion cropped up again whenever her heart was broken in love, whenever the life of a lesbian seemed impossible to endure a moment longer. But always in the past some buried instinct of self-preservation came to her in the nick of time and saved her. Once, in the private school, she went so far as to draw a razor blade over her wrists. But all she got out of the attempt was a minor wound that cleared up in a week; the sight of her blood had caused her to faint before any real damage could be done.

But now . . . now was the time. There would be no bloodshed, nothing the least bit messy. There would, in fact, be no corpse to get in people's way. She would just walk out into the water until she was too far out to save herself.

Then she would drown.

She might float out or sink and rot in the middle of the sea. Perhaps the fish would eat her flesh—the thought sickened her for a moment until she decided that she couldn't care less about what happened to her once she was dead. Then again she might float back up on the beach, just another victim of drowning.

And she wondered to herself how many so-called deaths by drowning were nothing other than people like herself, people who had taken the easiest way out of an intolerable situation, people who just couldn't stand it any more.

She left the road and walked to the beach. The tide was coming in, the beach deserted. She walked up and down at the edge of the water, getting her last thoughts in order, clearing her tired mind and preparing it for an eternity of peaceful inactivity.

Then she walked back onto the sand and removed her clothes. It didn't make sense—undressing so that she wouldn't get her clothes wet while she was busy drowning herself. But she decided that it would be best to be comfortable, pleasantly comfortable without the encumbrance of clothing. And the picture of her dead body in the water was a better picture if it was naked than if it wore clothes.

Nude, she stood motionless on the beach for a long moment, listening to the lapping of the surf and the indescribable sounds that a sea makes at night. At long length she walked to the edge of the water and stepped into the sea. The water was icy, but she made herself keep on going.

The water was midway up her calves. Then it reached her knees.

She went on walking.

She had it all planned, every bit of it. She didn't want to chance changing her mind, as she had done with the razor blade. She was a very poor swimmer, and she knew that if she got a little ways out over her head and tired herself out she would be unable to get back in no matter how hard she tried. Once she was out a short distance it would be all over for her, and all the self-preservation in the world wouldn't preserve Madelaine Carr.

The water was up to her waist, then to her breasts. The freezing cold water on the nipples of her breasts was like an icicle piercing her spinal cord, but she kept going. She could endure it, especially since in a moment or two more there would be no more pain forever.

Forever.

Forever, she thought dimly, was a long time. She remembered a jazz musician, one of her few male friends, who had been talking about suicide. He was a drug addict—three times a day he gave himself an injection of heroin, shooting the white powder straight into the mainline, the main artery in his arm, mainlining it so that the opiate could hit home at once. Three times a day—and his life was a living hell.

"Death," he had said, rolling the word on his tongue. "Death is a long gig."

And simultaneously she remembered the story of the old philosopher explaining Life and Death to a crowd of younger men.

"Life," the old man said, "is no better than Death."

"Then we should all kill ourselves," suggested one of the younger men.

The old man shook his head. "Death," he said gently, "is no better than Life."

She laughed bitterly to herself. The old man had obviously never been a lesbian. If he had, he would have been aware of the superiority of Death.

The water was neck-deep now and wading was becoming difficult. She floated and began to swim out to sea. The moon's reflection on the water before her looked like a giant golden plate waiting for her to swim out and grab it up, and she swam clumsily, reaching out for the moon.

She didn't get very far out before she was unable to swim any farther. Her arms felt like two lead weights and she was beginning to find it difficult to breathe. She tried to touch bottom and found that she couldn't. She was out over her head.

The instinct rose up within her as she had expected it would. All of a sudden she didn't want to die. She wanted to go on living, to take her chance on happiness and to look for some way to make her peace with the world. Everything would be all right, she decided. She could stand anything, even life without Sheila, even a life without love. Everything would be perfectly all right. Except for one thing.

She was drowning.

She slashed the water furiously in an effort to stay afloat. Her arms refused to do what her brain was trying to tell them to do and she submerged once, the water pulling her down.

When she surfaced she cried for help. She shouted out into the air as loud as she could, screaming her little lungs out in a last violent effort to stay alive.

She went under a second time. Then she surfaced and screamed again.

Her voice was loud and desperate over the barren sea.

Sheila's eyes fell open. Her head ached dully and her mind was cluttered with clouds. She leaned her head over the side of the bed and vomited neatly upon the floor, not quite knowing what she was doing and not caring about it in the least. All she knew was that her stomach wanted to get rid of its contents, and she was all in favor of letting her poor little stomach have its way.

Why was she awake? She let her eyelids drop shut again and prepared to drift back off into a quiet and comfortable slumber.

Then she remembered. Something had wakened her before and then she had passed out again. What could it have been? She had trouble remembering.

Then it came to her. She had been lying in bed, all alone by herself, and somebody had been touching her and caressing her and making love to her. Then her eyes had opened and the face they had seen had been that of the lesbian, that girl whose name was Madelaine Carr.

Then she had gone back to sleep, and now she was awake again and remembering.

Had Madelaine Carr made love to her? It was, she decided, some crazy sort of a dream. She glanced around the room, her eyes open again, but there was no sign that anybody else had been present. She couldn't remember hanging up her clothes, and that was strange because she usually remembered everything. But she could have had such an insignificant act slip her mind without much trouble.

No, it had to have been a dream. Why she would dream of Madelaine Carr was beyond her, but she knew that dreams seldom made any great deal of sense. No, it was a dream, and to hell with all dreams.

Her eyes were closed again. Her head was settled upon her pillow.

She was asleep within seconds.

The boy was walking along the beach when he heard the first cry. He straightened up; then, thinking that it was nothing more than his imagination, he lowered his head and began walking once again along the stretch of sand.

Then he heard the second cry—a long, drawn out *Heeeeelpppp!* coming from way out in the sea. He didn't wait for a third cry.

In seconds he had stripped himself of all his clothing. Then he was running, dashing over the sand and into the surf, running out into the sea until it became too difficult to run any more.

He began swimming, his arms cutting through the water and pulling him farther out. His eyes scanned the sea for a trace of the person who had shouted but he saw nothing and nobody.

He kept on swimming.

A body surfaced. There was no shout this time and he thought that he might be too late. But he kept going, and after a few more strokes he overtook the girl.

She fought him with what strength she had left, fought him in the irrational way that a drowning person fights a rescuer. But he was still strong, untired by the swim, and she was weak from fighting to stay alive. Without much difficulty he turned her around and gripped her in a cross-chest carry, his left arm around her chest with his hand clutching the muscle below her shoulder while he swam with his right arm and held the girl above water with his hip.

Swimming back to land took him longer than it had taken him to swim out. Fortunately he was in good shape: his arm didn't get tired and his lungs held up perfectly. He was barely breathing hard by the time he got the girl up onto dry land.

She was limp as a rag doll and about as lively. Without thinking he stretched her out on the sand on her stomach, first pulling out her tongue so that she wouldn't choke on it. Then he began artificial respiration, going through motions that he had learned so well that it had been impossible to forget them, even though he had never before had any occasion to put them to use.

The girl began breathing by herself after about five minutes of artificial respiration. He continued for a few more minutes to make sure that her lungs would work by themselves. Then, when she was breathing normally but still unconscious, he got up from her and sat down in the sand a few feet away, waiting for her to regain consciousness and thank him properly. He walked over to where he had dropped his clothing and took a pack of cigarettes and a book of matches from his shirt. Then he settled himself in the sand and smoked in silence, aware for the first time that the girl was very naked and very beautiful, remembering for the first time how her bare breast had felt against his forearm when he had towed her in to shore.

When Madelaine woke up she wasn't altogether certain whether she was alive or not. She had discarded belief in an afterlife at about the same time that she had ceased to believe in God, but now she was not sure. The last thing she remembered was being about to drown. Now, unless she had died and gone to some sort of celestial or subterranean reward, she was lying naked and wet and dripping upon a beach.

"You awake finally?"

She looked over at the boy. He seemed familiar but she couldn't place him.

"Cripes," he said, "you were out kind of deep. Don't you know better than to swim alone at night?"

She blinked.

"What happened?"

"What happened? You damn near drowned—that's what happened. I had to chase in after you and pull you out, and even then you tried to drown the both of us."

Then she *was* alive. That was good, she decided. She was suddenly very glad that she hadn't managed to drown herself.

"Aren't you even going to thank me?"

"Thank you," she said automatically.

"How come you were way out there?"

"I was trying to kill myself."

"Huh?"

"I was trying to kill myself," she repeated.

"Well, I'm sorry if I stopped you from something you wanted to do—"

"No," she said. "I changed my mind."

"Pretty dangerous trick."

There didn't seem to be anything to say to that, so she didn't say anything.

"Hey," he said suddenly, looking at her with new recognition, "you know, I should have let you drown."

She stared at him.

"You don't remember me?"

She didn't.

"Take a good look."

She took a good look—then, realizing for the first time that they were both quite naked, she folded her arms over her breasts and crossed her legs in an effort to conceal herself from his glance.

He laughed. "Honey," he said, "I've seen about all there is to see of you. But don't you remember who I am?"

He looked increasingly familiar. But she still didn't remember who he was.

"I sure as hell remember you," he said. "It's not every little frail who threatens to kick me in the crotch."

And then she remembered him.

The boy who had saved her life was Bruce Ryerson.

•   •   •

When he stood up and walked toward her she averted her eyes from him, not wanting to look at him. But he kept coming closer, and then he was seated in the sand beside her. She cringed noticeably when his hand fastened on her ankle and kneaded her flesh.

"It's a lucky thing for you that you never got around to it," he remarked. "I don't swim very fast after I get kicked where you wanted to kick me."

She colored but didn't say anything.

"I don't think that was very nice of you."

"I'm sorry," she stammered.

"You ought to show how sorry you are," he told her, and there was a change in his voice. It was huskier now, huskier and drawn with passion.

She was frightened now.

His hand moved from her ankle, up her leg to her knee. Her legs were crossed and the muscles in them tightened convulsively. She wanted to get up and run away from him but she didn't know where to run to.

Besides, she was too weak to move.

"You ought to be nice to me now," he said. "You ought to prove how grateful you are."

She shook her head, not trusting herself to speak. She was terrified now, knowing full well what was coming and not knowing how to resist him.

His hand traced its way from her knee up her thigh until he was patting her waist.

He touched her breast and she cringed again.

"You're built nice enough," he said. "Nice tits, even if they are a little small. And you got one hell of a fine tail on you."

"*Please*—"

He took her hand and placed it on him and she wanted to scream. Her mouth even opened for a scream but no words came out. She drew her hand away as if he had leprosy or something worse.

"Look," he said roughly, "I had a hell of a long swim a few minutes ago. I saved your damned life, and if you think you're holding out on me you got another think coming. I'm getting mine, honey."

"Please—"

"C'mon," he said. "You're gonna get it one way or the other, honey. You might as well give in nice and easy. It'll save me some trouble and you'll make sure you don't get hurt. Because I'll hurt you if I have to, honey."

"No—"

She tried to resist him. She tried as hard as she could but there was nothing she could do. He was bigger than he was and stronger than she was, and she was so tired from nearly drowning that she was powerless against him. With one hand he caught her two wrists and held them over her head. Then, as if rape was an everyday occurrence for him, he forced her back down on the sand.

He didn't cover her mouth; he must have known instinctively that she was not going to scream. With his free hand he sent little darts of pain racing through her, hurting her where she was so tender.

She fought him every step of the way but it didn't do any good. She tried to keep her legs tight together but he managed to get one knee between hers. Then his free hand balled up into a fist and lashed into her soft stomach. She moaned in sheer agony and she was defenseless.

He took her like a stallion taking a captive mare. He had no thought of anything other than his own satisfaction and he used her terribly, hurting her more than she had ever been hurt before, more than she had dreamed a girl could be hurt.

He hadn't realized that she was a virgin. When he discovered the fact he drew in his breath sharply, but instead of the discovery making him more gentle with her it only excited him still further and made him rougher and more vicious toward her.

She was built small and the pain nearly tore her in half. She thought that it was going to last forever, that the world would stand on end while the boy raped her and raped her and raped her.

Finally it was over.

She stayed where she was while he dressed and disappeared into the night. She remained on the sand for a long time, aching and hurting, until finally the pain was too much for her and she passed out.

It was morning when she woke. She got up and dressed herself, wanting only to get as far from the beach as she could.

The sun blazed down on a patch of blood-red sand.

Chapter 11

It was mid-afternoon. Your cabin was clean now, as clean as a Buchanan Shack ever was. Your empty bourbon bottle was out in the trash barrel, your floor was swept, your clothes were put away and your dishes were washed. You had had a shower, brushed your teeth, eaten your breakfast and lunch, combed and brushed your hair and powdered your nose like a good little girl.

Now what did you do?

You sat on your hands, Sheila thought. You sat on your hands and stared off into the middle of nowhere and you dug things because they were real. You sat on your hands and stared into space, and you did this because you knew full well what would happen if you stopped sitting on your hands and staring into space.

You would go out and find a man.

Well, she thought, there were worse things than going out and finding a man. She could always follow through on that weird dream she had had last night and go out and find a woman. That would be a switch.

The memory of the dream still lingered with her. She could remember all too clearly how her eyes had opened to find Madelaine Carr making love to her. Of all the half-assed dreams to have! It would have been different if she were the dreaming type, but generally her mind was totally vacant from the moment she put her head on the pillow and dozed off to sleep. She didn't dream. Of course, she was dreaming all the time when she slept, she reflected. That was what the psychologists said—you were always dreaming, but you generally didn't remember it. You slept and dreamed, but because you didn't know that you were dreaming you thought you weren't.

To hell with it, she decided. If you didn't know you were dreaming, then you weren't dreaming. If a bell rang in the middle of the ocean and nobody heard it, was the bell really ringing?

To hell with it.

But that, she thought, left her approximately right back where she had started from.

Sitting on her hands.

Staring off into space.

And wishing for a man.

She stood up finally, stood up from the broken-down uncomfortable old colonial chair that she was about ready to break up for firewood already, stood up and wandered into the tiny bathroom. She washed and dried her face again, examining it in the mirror to make sure that it looked its best. She was wearing a pale blue off-the-shoulder blouse, very simple in style except for a few ruffles at the top, and the blouse let the top part of her breasts show.

Ordinarily a blouse like that wouldn't have gone well with a pair of blue jeans. But when Sheila was wearing the blouse and jeans the viewer was more than willing to make allowances. Women in slacks or pants or blue jeans generally make one of two impressions—they look either sexless or eminently beddable.

Sheila Paine looked eminently beddable. The blue jeans were tight enough so that they revealed the precise shape of those parts of her that they covered. When a woman is in the least misshapen, the result is horrible. When the woman is built like Sheila Paine, the result is on the magnificent side.

She knew this. She knew the impression she would create when she strolled down Commercial Street, knew how easy it would be for her to find the sort of man she was looking for. Just any man wouldn't do, not today. She wanted a strong man, somebody who would dominate her and make her feel meek and submissive.

She had wanted such a man often in the past. At such times she would have a craving to submit her will totally and completely to the will of another, to permit herself to be slapped and pummeled, even whipped on one occasion, letting the pain that ran its course through her body bring her its own kind of satisfaction.

The amateur psychologists loved to pin labels on that kind of urge. *Sadism, masochism*—it seemed to Sheila that every person in the world was labelled with one or another of their little labels and mounted sprawling like a beetle on a pin in some small boy's insect collection.

Well, they could shove their labels. She already had one label pinned to her: *nymphomaniac*. And since it was her firm conviction that no one person could properly support more than one vice at a time, she didn't care at all about the other labels.

Her craving for pain wasn't masochism as such. For one thing it wasn't the primary concern of her life; it came only after deep periods of depression similar to the one she had just drunk her way out of. In addition, it was the subjection rather than the actual physical pain that she yearned for at such times. Subjection and something else.

She could remember one time several months ago when she had been in that sort of a mood. The partner she found for herself was a thin, wiry man with piercing eyes, a man with a deep streak of true sadism lying close to the surface within him. He had taken her to a hotel room in one of the less pleasant sections of town and sat fully clothed in a chair while he forced her to remove her clothes.

Then he made her walk up and down the room, stark naked, made her dance around in a certain humiliating way, finally made her perform obscene exercises with the walking cane that he carried. Then, after all that, he removed his clothing and made love to her in a rather routine fashion upon the bed. There was no physical pain involved at all.

She found a man in a bar. The bar was on Commercial Street just a block or so from the Purple Oyster, a cave-like bar that was dark even in the middle of the afternoon. Couples sat at the low round tables drinking cold beer that was served in huge pitchers. Mostly men sat at the bar itself. They drank either beer or whiskey, and everybody in the place was doing a lot of drinking.

There are, basically, two sorts of bars in Provincetown, if you discount for the moment the gay joints and the frontier tourist traps. There are bars for drinking and bars for socializing. At the latter customers gather for a drink or two to take the edge off, followed either by singing or group babbling or a merry pick-up. In the drinking bars, getting happily fried in short order is the object all sublime, an object achieved in a short amount of time.

The Grotto was a drinking bar. Since women are less prone to do their heavier drinking before the setting of the sun, Sheila was somewhat conspicuous when she sauntered through the door and into the bar. The few couples for the most part ignored her, but she could feel the eyes of the men at the bar as heads turned and eyes roamed over the blouse and blue jeans.

She discounted the bulk of the eyes. She was looking for a special type of man and just any man would not do. One by one she crossed the starers off her list; one pair of eyes, however, could not be eliminated. One man was staring at her in a way that promised a good deal of what she was after.

She stared back at him.

The man was big—not too tall, but heavy-set with muscular arms and wide shoulders. He appeared to be in his late thirties and he looked as though he had lived hard for each of those years. A jagged scar divided the left side of an unshaven face. His eyes were the clear blue that is found only in newborn babies and confirmed rye-drinkers. His nose had been broken once and reset clumsily, with the result that it spilled to one side of his face.

In short, the man looked rough, the nail-chewing and bullet-spitting type. His clothing confirmed the impression—a blue denim shirt the was not quite big enough to cover his barrel chest without stretching, matching denim work trousers that had worn through in the knees and had been patched at least once.

But there was something more than physical about the man, and that was what convinced Sheila that she had found her playmate. His gaze, impudent and respectful, never wavered. When he turned from her casually and spilled a shot glass full of rye down his throat his casualness seemed very studied and deliberate, a purposeful challenge to her femininity.

She decided to answer the challenge.

The stool to the right of the man was empty. Sheila walked directly to it and sat down on it. She ordered bourbon-and-water, mixing the drink elaborately and drinking off half of it in the first swallow. Turning to look at the man, she saw that he had chosen to ignore her for the moment.

"Hello," she said.

He turned on his stool. He looked at her minutely, spending a little time regarding her face and the rest of the time studying her body. Then, without saying a word, he ordered another drink and drank it.

"I said hello."

He turned and looked at her again. "I heard you," he told her calmly.

"Well?"

"Well what?"

"You could answer me, couldn't you?"

"I'm sorry," he said, turning away from her once again. "I don't have anything to do with prostitutes."

"Your mother must be lonely."

A smile appeared on his face. "That was quick," he said. "You got a good line of patter."

"I'm good at other things, too."

"Yeah?" He didn't sound overly interested, but she knew that was part of the game.

"Yes."

"Like what?"

"Like what I do in bed."

"What do you do in bed?"

"Damn near anything."

"For how much?"

"I'm sorry," she said. "I've never paid a man and I don't intend to start now."

He laughed, obviously amused this time. Then his mood changed abruptly as he crooked a finger at the bartender for a refill. "You don't want me," he said.

"Don't be so sure."

"I'm rough on women," he said.

"I know."

"I'm a rough guy."

"I know that. Why do you think I picked you out?"

"You mean it shows?"

She nodded. "To me it does. But I guess I know what to look for."

"And you like what you see?"

"Yes."

He drank the liquor.

"Don't *you* like what you see?"

He looked at her again, even bolder and franker with his eyes this time.

"Well?"

"I like."

"Then let's go."

He looked dubious. "You sure you know what you're getting into?"

"You've got the mechanics mixed up," she told him. "I'm not

getting into anything, if you stop to think about it for a minute. It's the other way around."

He chuckled deep in his throat. "Let's go," he said.

When they were seated side by side in her convertible, she said: "My name's Sheila Paine, if it matters."

"It doesn't," he said.

"You might tell me yours."

"I might," he said. "Then again I might not."

She drove in silence.

"My name doesn't matter either," he said at length.

"Tell me anyway."

"Why?"

"I want to know."

"You keep a list of all the men you sleep with?"

"No," she said. "Not all of them. Just the ones that are worth making a note of."

"What makes you sure I'll be worth it?"

"I'm not at all sure," she said. "If you're not I can forget your name easily enough. If you are, I might not remember to ask you afterwards."

"That's true," he said.

But he still hadn't told her his name.

"Look," she said finally, annoyed with him for being such a nuisance and annoyed with herself for pressing the point, "why don't you just tell me your name?"

"Max," he said.

"Do you have a last name, too?"

"Bell."

"Max Bell," she said.

"Will that do?"

"Yes," she said, "it'll do."

She parked the car in her parking place and locked it. Inside the cabin he took his time looking around, getting the feel of the place, while she stood awkwardly to one side. She was unsure of herself now, not knowing just what he expected her to do. She thought for a moment that it was time for her to start taking off her clothes, then decided that she would wait until he gave her some idea of what he wanted.

He walked around the cabin, inspecting it. "Dumpy joint," he said. "Couldn't you afford anything better?"

She didn't answer.

"Just wanted a place to fornicate in, huh?"

She shrugged.

He turned to her.

"Strip," he said.

She stripped. She pulled the blouse loose from the dungarees and hauled it over her head, dropping it to the wooden floor of the cabin. Reaching around behind her she unhooked the bra and peeled it off.

She was strangely unmoved as she unbelted the dungarees and stepped out of them. He was looking at her almost coldly and her own feelings were equally cool. When her panties were off and she stood naked before him she didn't know what to feel any more than she knew what to do.

"Come here," he said.

She walked closer to him. She kept walking until she was less than a foot from him. Then she stopped and stood unmoving while his eyes travelled the length of her body.

"Not bad," he said.

She didn't answer.

One of his hands encircled one of her arms. She looked down and saw that his hand was huge, with long thick fingers and swollen knuckles. The veins stood up on the back of his hand.

His grip tightened.

He was squeezing her arm hard and jets of pain went through her. Her knees buckled and her lips parted for a groan of pain but no sound came from between them. She felt nothing but the pain, an overwhelming and excruciating pain that sent the blood rushing to her brain.

But no flood of excitement accompanied the pain.

He let go of her as abruptly as he had begun to squeeze it. He stood for a moment, looking as though he was about to say something.

Then he hit her.

He didn't ball his hand into a fist. Instead he hit her with his open palm, slapping her full in the face. It was a hard, powerful slap, delivered with the full force of his strong arm behind it, and it lifted her from her feet and sent her half-flying for several feet before she fell to the floor. Her face stung from the blow and her eyes clouded automatically with tears.

Pain.

No excitement.

She remained seated on the floor, her legs outstretched behind her and her knees bent. She looked at him, wondering what was coming next.

"Get up."

She got to her feet.

"Come here."

She approached him until she stood closer to him than before. She could feel the angry red welt on her cheek; looking downward, she could see that her breast was already black and blue when he had squeezed her.

His right hand reached out and touched her stomach, then probed lower. She felt everything that he was doing to her while remaining strangely unmoved by the whole procedure. She watched dispassionately as the fingers of his right hand curled to form a fist. He drew the fist back and she continued to watch with the same cold stare. She didn't even prepare herself by tensing her muscles to receive the blow.

He hit her below the belt.

Hard.

Her legs folded up and she went to her knees, her hands clutching herself where he had hit her as if their touch would relieve the pain. For a moment she couldn't breathe; then she couldn't see either and a moment later she had to keep her eyes closed to keep from blacking out. Her stomach felt as though it had been stepped on by an elephant that was carrying another elephant.

She didn't make a sound.

"Get up."

She tried to get up. She got her hands and feet in position and tried to raise herself to a standing position. She didn't make it.

Then he was at her side, one hand under each arm. He helped her to her feet and didn't let go of her when she was standing but led her gently to the bed. His manner was in such pronounced contrast to the violence of a moment earlier that she wanted to ask him what was responsible for the change. But she couldn't get the words out over the pain.

He made her sit down on the edge of the bed, then sat down next to her. It took her a moment to realize that he wasn't about to make love to her. Instead he sat with his hands folded on his lap, his eyes gazing thoughtfully across the small room.

She waited.

Finally he said: "This is no good."

She was silent.

"No good," he repeated. "I'm not getting any kick out of it and neither are you."

She breathed deeply. The pain was diminishing now and she was able to think clearly. He was right, she decided. The pain and punishment and subjection was what she had wanted, but it wasn't having the desired effect, not in the least.

"Right?"

She nodded.

"Did I hurt you?"

"Yes," she said softly.

"Very much?"

She nodded.

"I'm sorry," he said. "I meant to hurt you, of course. I thought that was what we both wanted. But it isn't working out right."

She nodded again, agreeing with him.

"I think I'll go now," he said. "Unless there's anything else you want."

She shook her head soundlessly.

She watched him leave, his heavy, broad-shouldered form looking somehow less impressive now than it had when she had first seen him. He made his way to the door and vanished through it, and she thought that it would be a fairly long walk for him back to the bar.

For a moment she considered offering to give him a lift, then rejected the thought. She wanted to be alone.

She was disturbed, very disturbed, by what had just taken place. It was as though she didn't have the slightest idea what she wanted—Max Bell hadn't been the answer, and she was nowhere close to knowing what the answer was. There was a hunger within her, but she was unsure what it was a hunger for and what had caused it.

She dressed again, taking more time putting the clothes on than she had taking them off. Then she sat down again on the edge of the bed, patting her stomach gingerly where it hurt and thinking to herself.

She wished briefly that the bourbon bottle wasn't empty. Then she decided that even getting drunk wouldn't do her much good.

She was sitting like that, on the edge of the bed, when Madelaine Carr walked into the cabin.

CHAPTER 12

The girl looked even smaller and meeker than Sheila remembered her. Her face was very pale and she seemed to be completely open and defenseless. Her eyes were vacant and unblinking, her lips bloodless.

"Can I—"

"Come inside," Sheila said. The girl walked into the cabin, looking about hesitantly. Sheila indicated the chair with a wave of her hand and Madelaine sat down.

"It's funny," Sheila was saying. "Any other day but today I would have thrown you out if you so much as showed your face here. But today I'm almost glad to see you. I don't know why."

Madelaine nodded, as if she understood.

"What do you want?"

Madelaine was nervous. "I came here because I . . . I have a confession to make. That sounds rather banal, doesn't it? But that's what I have to do."

"Go ahead."

"I . . . could I have a cigarette?"

Sheila passed the pack to the girl and watched her take out a cigarette and light it. She took a puff and expelled the smoke without inhaling it first.

"You don't smoke much, do you?"

"I never smoke. But I'm so terribly nervous that I thought a cigarette might help me relax."

Sheila nodded.

Madelaine took another puff of the cigarette. "The confession," she said. "Silly way to put it, isn't it? It makes one think of going to a priest, and you don't exactly remind one of a priest."

"I guess not."

Madelaine was silent again. Then she said: "I came to your cabin last night."

Silence.

"I came to your cabin. I knocked but nobody answered, and I tried the door and it was open. I came inside."

"I see."

"You were lying on the floor. You were unconscious and I believe you had taken quite a bit of whiskey."

"Bourbon," Sheila said. "I drank a fifth of it."

Madelaine nodded. "I was afraid you would catch a cold," she said. "I undressed you and put you to bed."

"I see."

"And then . . . then I—"

"Go on."

"Then I made love to you."

Sheila closed her eyes. "I thought it was a dream," she said. "I was sure it was a dream."

"Then you remember?"

"Not really. I remember waking up and seeing you but I thought . . . I was certain it was a dream."

"It wasn't a dream."

"I guess not."

"It was wrong," Madelaine said. "It was something I'll probably be ashamed of for the rest of my life. It was a vile thing to do."

Sheila didn't say anything.

"I had to tell you," Madelaine went on. "I couldn't just leave it like that. I'm not the type of person who makes a habit of . . . of seducing other women while they sleep. No matter what you may think of me—and I know that you don't think much of me— no matter what, I wanted you to know that what happened last night is something that has never happened before."

Sheila nodded, feeling much calmer than she thought possible. She looked at the little girl, saw the lines of tension in her face, noticed the cigarette that was burning by itself between the second and third fingers of Madelaine's small right hand.

"I suppose I'd better go now," Madelaine said. "I won't bother you any more."

She started to stand up.

"Wait a minute."

She sat down again.

"That wasn't all," Sheila said. "You must have had more reason than that for coming to see me again."

The girl hesitated.

"Tell me about it."

"All right—I did have another reason. I'm still in love with you, Sheila. I think I'll always be in love with you."

"And—"

"And . . . and I want you to be in love with me. I wanted to talk with you, explain things to you. I didn't know if you would listen to me, but I had to try."

Sheila closed her eyes again, considering. She was unsure why she was taking the time and trouble to listen to the girl, thinking that it might be a result of the failure of her affair with Max Bell. But, whatever the reason, she felt that it was only fair to hear the girl out.

"Go ahead," she said. "I'll listen to you."

"I'm glad," Madelaine said. "I . . . I love you, Sheila. But you know that already."

Sheila nodded.

"I think you could let yourself love me, if you gave yourself a chance."

"I don't think that's possible," Sheila said. "I know that everybody's supposed to have a certain amount of latent homosexuality inside, but I guess I'm about as heterosexual a woman as there is. You know what I am, Madelaine."

"Tell me."

"I'm a nymphomaniac."

"Does that make you so . . . so heterosexual?"

"Doesn't it?"

"I don't think so, Sheila."

Sheila waited for her to go on.

"Sheila, I think . . . I think that you are lesbian. Wait, let me explain that statement. I think that everything about you, every facet of your personality, every sexual action in your life, has been an attempt to repress your lesbianism. I—"

"That's impossible."

"See? You've been listening to me very carefully, but as soon as I try to tell you exactly what you are, then you bristle and try to deny it."

"I'm trying to deny it because it's not true."

"Are you so certain?"

"Of course—" She broke off suddenly, not so certain all of a sudden. What Madelaine was trying to tell her was too much for her to begin to accept, and something within her made her want to shout and scream that it was not true. But she forced herself to remain silent and to hear what the other girl had to say.

"Sheila, you told me a minute ago that you're a nymphomaniac. How many men have you had relations with?"

"Too many—I couldn't tell you just how many there were."

"And did you find these relations satisfactory?"

"I enjoyed them, if that's what you mean."

"That's not what I mean."

"What *do* you mean?"

"Did you reach orgasm?"

It took her a few seconds to get out the word *No.*

"Have you ever had an orgasm?"

This time she just shook her head.

Madelaine nodded once, then shifted to another track.

"Do you remember the first time you met me?"

"At the party, that party at the Hookery?"

"That's right."

"I remember."

"Do you remember what you did after you met me?"

"How could I forget?"

Madelaine smiled sadly. "Don't you think there's a connection between meeting me and what came afterwards? Don't you see some sort of a relationship?"

"I'm not sure I understand what you mean."

The cigarette started to burn Madelaine's fingers and she looked about the room for a place to put it. Sheila indicated an ashtray and the smaller girl put out the cigarette in the tray. Then she sat down again.

"Suppose for a moment that I'm right," she said. "Suppose for the time being that I'm correct in my analysis and that you are a repressed lesbian."

"All right."

"Now look at it from this standpoint—you come to the party with a man. You meet me, and unconsciously you sense what I am and what I represent. You want to fight what I stand for. So what method do you choose?"

"Oh. But—"

"Do you see?" Madelaine's voice rose with excitement. "Do you see what I'm driving at? You had to prove to yourself that you were a woman because you felt yourself drawn to me!"

"I don't know," Sheila said. "I don't know if I can accept that."

"*Can* accept it? Or *want* to accept it?"

She didn't say anything.

"Of course you don't want to accept it," Madelaine said. "Nobody does. When you're a lesbian you can't live a normal life. You don't have a husband or children. Society doesn't accept you, because society is afraid of homosexuality as you are right now. But you've got to make a choice, Sheila. You have to come to a decision. You have to ask yourself whether what you have right now is preferable to what you would have if you . . . changed over. You don't have a normal life the way things stand, do you?"

"No. No, I don't."

"Do you have any hope for that kind of life, with husband and children and a family?"

She thought briefly of Harvey Chase. He had wanted to marry her, to give her a home and children. "No," she said. "No, I don't have any hope for that kind of life."

"Then I think you ought to listen to me."

"I'm listening."

Madelaine fumbled for another cigarette. She was plainly nervous now and she had trouble getting the cigarette lit. She drew deeply on it, still not inhaling, and it was comical the way she puffed on the cigarette and blew the smoke out all at once.

"Have you ever loved a man, Sheila?"

"No."

"I didn't think so. You don't even like men very much, do you? You don't like them as people."

"I suppose you're right."

"You hate them, don't you? You actually hate them—not all of them, perhaps, but the bulk of them."

"Maybe."

"Of course you do. You've been trying to get even with them—why else do you think you've slept with so many of them? You've been taking everything out of the men, fighting them with the one weapon at your command. You've been using your body as a weapon, Sheila."

Sheila closed her eyes again, trying to digest what the girl was saying.

"Look at me, Sheila."

The words were a command. Sheila opened her eyes and took a long look at the girl who was sitting so prim and proper in the uncomfortable chair. It was as if she were seeing her for the first time—seeing the smooth and clear skin that was as pure and white as ivory, seeing the fine features and the slender body, seeing the small perfect breasts and trim waistline. She looked the girl over very thoroughly and Madelaine almost turned red under her close scrutiny.

"How do I look to you, Sheila?"

"You're . . . very beautiful."

"Do you find me attractive?"

"I . . . I don't know."

"Pretend for a moment that you are a lesbian, Sheila. Now look at me—do you find me attractive?"

"I . . . yes, I think so."

"Would you like to kiss me?"

She couldn't answer.

"All right—let's go a little slower. Would you like me to sit next to you?"

"I—"

"Would you, Sheila?"

"If you want to."

"It's not what *I* want, Sheila. It's what *you* want. Would you like me to sit next to you?"

"All right." Her voice was very soft and she could hardly recognize it.

Madelaine stood up. Her body was liquid in motion as she walked the few steps to the bed and sat down beside the blonde girl. Their bodies were very close but there was no contact between them. Even without the actual physical contact Sheila could sense the nearness of the dark-haired girl. She was calm and tense all at once, unable to understand the feelings that were going through her.

Was Madelaine right? Could she be right? Was she really a lesbian, and was all her life nothing but a protest against a condition she was unwilling to accept? She didn't know, and she felt as though her mind was going around in ever diminishing concentric circles.

"Sheila—"

She turned and looked at the girl.

"Now would you like me to kiss you?"

"I—"

Madelaine shook her head suddenly. "No," she said, "let me change that. Would you like to kiss me?"

Her head swam.

"Tell me, Sheila. Would you like that? I'm here for you, Sheila. You don't have to say a word if you don't want to. You don't have to tell me anything. All you have to do is kiss me, my darling. All you have to do is take me in your arms and kiss me."

She couldn't breathe, couldn't speak a word. The nearness of Madelaine was like strong wine and she could only let her body respond instinctively, could only permit herself to do what she had to do.

Her hands reached for the girl. She took Madelaine's face between her hands, one hand on each soft cheek. Slowly, mechanically, she brought the girl's lovely face close to her own while Madelaine let herself be drawn in closer to Sheila.

"Go ahead, Sheila." She was whispering intensely, her eyes shut now and her lips close together. "Go ahead, my darling. Do what you want to do."

Then she kissed Madelaine. Her lips were warm and soft upon the warm and soft and pale lips of the smaller girl, her hands gentle on the sides of Madelaine's face. The kiss was brief and not a passionate kiss. It was over almost as quickly as it had begun. A second later she released Madelaine and the two girls were sitting side by side once again.

"You liked that, Sheila."

It was a statement, not a question. And it was a true statement.

"Did you enjoy kissing boys when you were younger, Sheila? I'll bet you didn't go in much for necking, did you?"

"I never had a chance. I started going all the way before I was old enough to neck."

"You still could have necked, as a prelude to intercourse if nothing else. But you didn't like it, did you?"

"No," she said honestly. "I just wanted to hurry up and get started with the main event."

"And you didn't enjoy kissing?"

"Not especially."

"But you liked it right now, didn't you?"

She nodded, unable to speak.

"Kiss me again," she said. "Kiss me the way you want to kiss me. Go ahead."

Again Sheila's hands framed Madelaine's face. Again she brought the girl close to her and pressed her own lips against Madelaine's.

This time the kiss took longer. Madelaine's mouth opened under the gentle pressure of Sheila's tongue. Sheila's lips crossed Madelaine's mouth and her tongue slipped between the two pale lips, tasting the richness of the girl's lips and tongue, tasting and caressing and making love.

The kiss ended.

"Oh Madelaine."

"Do you see what I mean?"

"Yes, I see."

"How do you feel, Sheila?"

"I can't describe it."

"It's different than you've ever felt before, isn't it? Have you felt like this with a man?"

"Not exactly."

"How is it different?"

"I . . . I'm not sure."

Madelaine took Sheila's hand and held it between her own two hands. She raised it to her lips, pressing moist kisses against the palm and rubbing her cheek against it. Then, reluctantly, she returned Sheila's hand to the blonde girl's lap.

"But it is different."

"Yes—it's very different."

"Do you feel excited?"

"In a way."

"But not desperately excited. You enjoy what we're doing and you'd like it to go on, but if it stopped now it wouldn't tear you up inside. It's not the hectic type of excitement you feel with a man. Am I right?"

"You're right."

The girl smiled. She was winning now, and she knew that she was winning, and she was smiling with the sureness of a lover who was no longer to be denied complete possession of a loved one.

"Do you see, Sheila? This is the kind of love you were made for, my darling. Your body realizes this. That's why your body is taking its time."

Her arms went around the girl. Her hands gripped Madelaine's shoulders and drew her close.

Bare breasts touched bare breasts in an embrace that was something Sheila had never known before. Her whole body began to tingle with genuine anticipation. Her breasts felt alive in a way they had never felt in the past. Her whole body seemed to want to sing with joy and beauty and happiness and love.

They kissed, mouth tasting mouth, tongue saying hello to tongue, body giving joy and pleasure to body.

They drew apart.

"Sheila?"

"Yes—"

"What are you, Sheila?"

"I'm—"

"Tell me, my darling."

"I'm a lesbian."

"How do you feel, darling?"

"I feel wonderful."

"Have you ever felt this way before, darling?"

"Never."

"Do you want me, Sheila?"

"Forever."

"How do you feel about me, darling?"

Silence for a moment, a long moment in which the two of them looked deep into each other's eyes.

Then: "I love you, Madelaine."

Madelaine's eyes flooded with joy and happiness and love. And then she said: "Now I'm going to love you, darling. Now I'm going to show you what the world is. I'm going to show you everything, darling."

CHAPTER 13

Madelaine's kisses were turning her into a raging inferno, burning her up and tearing her apart until Madelaine became the only thing that mattered, the only thing in the entire world that was of the slightest importance.

The sun stood still for a moment, then blacked out completely. Time stopped and day turned into night and back into day again. The waters rose up out of the sea and splashed across the sky, the sky turned every color of the rainbow and swept down to engulf the earth, and the whole world burned with an iridescent blue flame. She was beyond thinking, beyond feeling, beyond existing as an independent entity. She was a part of Madelaine and Madelaine became a part of her and that was all that mattered. Then all at once she realized what was happening to her and she threw back her head to cry for the sheer joy of it.

But she couldn't make a sound.

It was happening. She could feel it starting deep within her very being and moving outward, spreading through her veins and arteries and capillaries, spreading all through her as she moved higher . . .

Still higher . . .

Upward and outward, downward and inward, with the world

spinning and all the world whirling like a dervish, and oh oh oh, it was actually happening! happening!

Up to the top.

Then down, down, down, deeper and deeper in a descent that was faster than the speed of light, faster than fast, faster than anything could possibly happen.

Down.

To the very bottom of the world.

And to the incredible indescribable peace she had never before found.

The peace she had been seeking for her entire life.

"It . . . it happened."

"I told you it would."

"It happened to me. I . . . I climaxed."

"Of course. Didn't you know that you would?"

"I suppose I had given up hoping."

"You don't have to give up now. It will always happen for us, Sheila. Always."

"Every time?"

"Every single time."

She sighed. She was too weak to move, too weak to do anything but love and be happy, sublimely happy and finally completely relaxed. She smiled.

"I love you," she told Madelaine.

"Tell me about it."

"I love you," she repeated. "I love you so much I can't see straight."

"And you liked what I did to you?"

"Do you have to ask?"

Madelaine smiled.

"What will we do now, Maddy? Where do we go from here?"

"How do you mean?"

"I mean . . . well, what'll we do?"

"We'll live together."

"Where?"

Madelaine considered. "I think right here will be best," she said. "My landlady might catch on and get somewhat upset, and besides this cottage is rented by the season. I can move out of my room whenever I want."

"That's not what I mean."

"No? What *do* you mean then?"

"I took it for granted that we'd live together for the rest of the summer. I mean after the summer's over, what'll we do then? Will you still want to be with me or won't you want me anymore?"

"I'll always want you, silly."

"Then—"

"We'll just live together, darling. Isn't that simple enough? We'll get an apartment together and live together and make love until we can't see straight any more. All night and all day—it'll be a wonder if we get any work done, but we'll have fun, darling."

"Do you mean it?"

"Of course I mean it."

Sheila smiled. "You'll . . . keep on wanting me?"

"Forever."

"Forever is a long time," Sheila said, and Madelaine smiled remembering how she had said those same words to herself before she had tried to commit suicide. And she was so glad she had been saved, glad even if she had been forced to go through what she went through with Bruce Ryerson. It was worth it.

Because now she was happier—far happier—than she had ever been in her life.

"Forever isn't long enough to love you properly," she said.

"You already loved me properly."

"I did?"

"Yes—very properly."

"I thought it was pretty improper, baby."

Sheila giggled.

They were on the bed together. Sheila's head was settled on the small pillow, her body curled contentedly like that of a giant cat by a fireside. Madelaine was beside her, her head level with Sheila's shoulder, one arm draped over Sheila's back. With her hand she rubbed the small of Sheila's back and the nape of her neck, her hand moving lazily.

"Maddy?"

"What is it, baby?"

"Where will we live?"

"I don't know—where do you want to live?"

"Boston?"

"Maybe. But it might do us good to get away from Boston. I know a lot of people there that I'd just as soon not see again."

"Me too."

"How about New York?"

"How about it?"

"You ever been there?"

"Not for very long."

"Would you like to live there, baby?"

"I think so."

"It might be a good idea," Madelaine said. "You're a gay girl now, you know."

"I know."

"And you've got to start thinking like a gay girl, Sheila. You won't be able to lead a normal life any more, honey. Not now."

"I've never led a normal life."

"It'll be less normal now."

"It won't be so bad."

"I know."

Silence for a long time. They were both lost in their own thoughts, lost in new love, lost in love for each other. The room was very silent.

"Maddy—"

"What, darling?"

"Maddy, I want to . . . to do it to you."

"To do *what* to me?"

She couldn't answer.

"Sheila—"

"What you did to me, Maddy. I want to do the same for you."

"Oh."

"Don't you want—"

"Of course, sugar. But are you sure you want to?"

"I'm sure."

"I mean . . . well, some girls don't like to do it right away. It takes them awhile to get used to the idea. If you want to wait—"

"I don't want to wait."

"You see, I don't want to rush you, Sheila. Sometimes it takes some time."

"You're not rushing me."

"It's just that—"

"Maddy," she said, her voice drawn suddenly, "I'm in love with you. Can't you understand? I'm in love with you and I want to make love to you."

"Oh, honey!"

Sheila sat up on the bed, very sure of herself now, surer than she had ever been before. Madelaine started to sit up also but Sheila's hands gripped her shoulders and lowered her gently but firmly to the bed.

"Now it's your turn to lie still," she told her. "You be passive this time and let me love you. It's my turn now, Maddy."

A smile blossomed on Madelaine's face. "There's a way we can both be active at once," she said softly. "Remind me to show it to you sometime."

"I think I know what it is."

"Do you want to try it?"

"Not now."

"Are you sure?"

"Later," Sheila said. "There'll be time."

"Time for everything."

"That's right. Now close your eyes."

Obediently Madelaine closed her eyes. Sheila sat gazing down at her, her eyes taking in the startling beauty of the little girl. It was all so confusing—in some ways she felt years and years older than Madelaine; in other ways she felt that she was a little girl and Maddy was a mother to her. But she decided that it all didn't matter a damn. They loved each other—that was what mattered.

She kissed Maddy's lips, her chin, her throat. As she did so she was surprised to discover that she was receiving as much pleasure from exciting Madelaine as she had received when Madelaine had been doing those things to her, and when Madelaine began to breathe hard. Sheila's breathing increased in the same way.

Perhaps that was what love was, she thought in a flash. Maybe that was what made all the difference—the ability to take pleasure in the pleasure of another, to get your kicks from the kicks of the one you loved.

But she stopped thinking.

She was too busy.

She began kissing Madelaine's breasts the way Madelaine had kissed hers. Madelaine's breasts were sweet and she loved them very much, just as she loved the way that her kisses were driving Madelaine into a passionate state, making the girl's fingers tighten into little fists, making the tendons in her legs as tight as drumheads.

Tenderly, lovingly, she kissed all there was to kiss of Madelaine. At the end, when she gave Madelaine the caress that brought her to the peak, her own heart flowed over with love and pleasure.

Madelaine was in her arms then, soft and weak and wet with her own tears. Sheila felt better than she had ever felt in her life, good and beautiful inside, happy and content and relaxed.

They slept.

When they awoke they made love again in the manner Madelaine had spoken of before, with each of them taking both an active and a passive role. It was good, wonderful in fact, and after it was over they lay for a long time in bed, sharing a cigarette or two and talking of their love. Then Madelaine dressed, taking Sheila's car to pick up her clothes so that she could move in with Sheila.

Alone, Sheila had her thoughts to keep her company. She wondered how it would turn out, this new love affair that the two of them shared. Madelaine had told her of the short duration of most lesbian experiences, and she could only hope that their own affair would prove to be an exception to the general rule.

Forever, Madelaine had said.

Forever *was* a long time, no matter what. But they could try; living together in New York it very well might work out.

And no matter what happened in the future, for the time being they had each other. For the time being it was warm and sunny in Provincetown and the beach was flat and white and sandy.

And they were together.

And that was enough.

My Newsletter: I get out an email newsletter at unpredictable intervals, but rarely more often than every other week. I'll be happy to add you to the distribution list. A blank email to lawbloc@gmail.com with "newsletter" in the subject line will get you on the list, and a click of the "Unsubscribe" link will get you off it, should you ultimately decide you're happier without it.

Lawrence Block has been writing award-winning mystery and suspense fiction for half a century. You can read his thoughts about crime fiction and crime writers in *The Crime of Our Lives*, where this MWA Grand Master tells it straight. His most recent novels are *The Girl With the Deep Blue Eyes*; *The Burglar Who Counted the Spoons*, featuring Bernie Rhodenbarr; *Hit Me,* featuring Keller; and *A Drop of the Hard Stuff,* featuring Matthew Scudder, played by Liam Neeson in the film *A Walk Among the Tombstones*. Several of his other books have been filmed, although not terribly well. He's well known for his books for writers, including the classic *Telling Lies for Fun &f Profit,* and *The Liar's Bible.* In addition to prose works, he has written episodic television (*Tilt!*) and the Wong Kar-wai film, *My Blueberry Nights*. He is a modest and humble fellow, although you would never guess as much from this biographical note.

Email: lawbloc@gmail.com
Twitter: @LawrenceBlock
Facebook: lawrence.block
Website: lawrenceblock.com

www.ingramcontent.com/pod-product-compliance
Lightning Source LLC
Chambersburg PA
CBHW061137200626
46817CB00016B/1721